WARY PARTNERS

J.L. Guin

Wary Partners
Copyright © 2021 by Jerry L. Guin
Cover Design Livia Reasoner
Sundown Press
www.sundownpress.com

All rights reserved.
ISBN: 9798781880973

This is a work of fiction. The characters, incidents, and dialogues are products of the author's imagination and are not to be construed as real.

No part of this book may be used or reproduced in any manner whatsoever without written permission of the publisher, except in the case of brief quotations embodied in critical articles and reviews.

CHAPTER ONE

Great Bend, in mid-state Kansas, so named for its location of the great bend of the Arkansas River where the river course turns eastward then southeast, was put on the map in 1872 when the Atchison, Topeka and Santa Fe railroad laid its tracks through the quiet, growing town. A year later, Great Bend became a shipping point for cattle coming up from Texas. This transformed the city into a rowdy—often times violent—cow town.

After the herds arrived at the shipping pens then were loaded onto railcars, the herd drovers received their pay for the work. As many of the regular ranch hands left town, they would most likely be accompanying the owner and returning prized remuda horseflesh and chuckwagons to their home ranch.

Those who were not regular hands but had signed on for the duration of drive *only*, either left town in search of employment or began celebrating the end of their daylight-to-midnight watching over the jumpy cattle during the drive.

Nineteen-year-old Larry Creed was sitting at a table in Milt's Saloon along with Lanie Brooks, a young soiled dove.

Larry and his two brothers, Marcus and Wayne, had begun celebrating yesterday. Their father, Thomas Creed, owner of the T.C. Creed Ranch from southern Texas, had given each of his sons a fifty-dollar bonus for their help in getting the ranch's herd to market.

"Go and have yourselves some fun, boys. You earned it!" he had proclaimed.

Larry was unused to the effects of alcohol, and his body reacted after too many drinks. He had finished off last night's revelry by violently regurgitating the contents of his stomach.

The next morning in their shared hotel room, his brother, Wayne, laughed and said, "Guess you found out that the bottle bites!" He added, "I've found that the best cure is to take a shot or two of the same stuff you guzzled last night. Once you get past that first shot, you'll feel better afterward."

When Larry's two brothers headed toward a nearby café, Larry declined. He was in such misery that he decided to take Wayne's advice. It was 8:00 a.m. when Milt's Saloon opened for business. Larry immediately went inside and stepped to the bar.

Owner Milt Stubbs stood behind the bar. "You look like you need a little hair of the dog that bit you!" He grinned. "I have just the thing to fix you up." He turned, took a tall glass, and filled it half full of tomato juice, then took hold of a bottle of clear liquid and filled the glass. He added a little pepper then set the drink before Larry.

Larry looked at the concoction, then nodded. He took the glass in hand and sipped. He figured he'd get sick again, but instead, it didn't taste as bad as he'd expected. He upended the glass and drank three swallows. When it went down without a hitch, he drank the rest. He began to feel better immediately.

"That was pretty good, Milt. I'll have another."

Wayne and Marcus showed up around ten o'clock. The three brothers took drinks and a bottle to a nearby table. Marcus spoke up. "Hell, boy, I thought we was gonna have to get you to a doctor, sick as you were last night. Might want to get something to eat and take it easy today. Wayne and I got a pair of womenfolk from next door lined up for a picnic this afternoon. I figure we'll be tied up most of the day, so you'll be on your own. You ought to rest up. The old man said we'd be leaving first thing tomorrow, heading home—and you don't want to be riding out all hung over."

Larry knew that was good advice from his older brother. But after the two had left when the bottle was empty, Larry was feeling good and decided one more drink wouldn't hurt.

It was close to eight that night when George Wiggins, wearing a black claw hammer suit coat, string tie, and whipcord trousers tucked into knee-high shiny, black boots came to stand in front of the table where Larry was seated with the same soiled dove he'd occupied himself with the night before.

The man extended a hand to the young woman. "Come with me, Lanie. You've wasted near to two hours on this fella, time to move on. Now, I got a man with jingle in his pocket waiting, wants to see you real bad."

Lanie stared at the man, then rose to her feet. Larry Creed was not feeling any pain, but he was not drunk. After suffering the misery of last night's unrestricted drinking, he had been nursing his few drinks all day, just taking a sip now and then, knowing that hitting the saddle in the morning, the old man would expect him to be sharp. But he didn't like the fancy-dressed man thinking he could just walk up and take the girl away while she was sitting with him. What the hell? He'd bought her a couple of drinks already.

Larry jumped to his feet. "Wait a minute! She's with me. Go find yourself another girl!"

The suited man remained calm and extended a placating hand palm down in an effort to get Larry to relax. He spoke in a smooth, even voice. "Lanie's a working girl. She needs to circulate, and now, she has a paying customer waiting for her."

Larry didn't care what the reasoning of the intrusion was—it just hit him the wrong way. He had already spent plenty of money buying the girl her watered-down drinks and figured to end up in her crib before the night was over, and now this rude joker had showed up and was spoiling his fun.

Larry pointed a finger at the stranger. His other hand rested on the handle of his holstered .45 Colt. "You get the hell away from here, mister, 'fore I drill ya!" It was a lame threat, to see if the intruder would step away.

Larry really was not that good with his six-gun. He wore a .45 Colt in a holster belted to his side because all the other drovers, including his brothers, wore one. He had never shot at anything other than wild game or targeted cans and bottles.

Lanie quickly stepped to stand behind Larry as he faced

George Wiggins.

The man replied, "Take it easy, fella. Tell you what…I'll buy you a drink to show there are no hard feelings." He reached a hand inside his jacket for his wallet. Larry was so angry he had not paid any attention to what the man had offered.

All Larry saw was the man's hand going into the inside of his suit jacket, and he figured the man was going for a hidden handgun. Larry quickly palmed his six-gun and brought it up, the muzzle pointed toward Wiggins. He had automatically cocked the weapon and had his finger on the trigger. He did not intend to shoot the man. Having never used the weapon to settle a dispute, he had drawn his six-gun as a showing that he wouldn't be trod upon, in hopes that his action would be enough to make the man retreat without himself feeling like a soft-soap for allowing the intrusion.

Then, something happened that would forever change his life. From behind the young drover, Lanie Brooks suddenly reached out and pushed against his arm. The push was hard enough to cause his already tightened finger to move slightly and fire the six-gun. Unfortunately, the bullet from the unintended shot hit the suited man in the middle of his chest, splitting his breastbone and nipping a corner of the man's heart, killing him instantly.

Larry watched, wide-eyed, through the gun smoke, as the man, his shirtfront leaking large amounts of blood, crumpled to the floor.

He stared disbelievingly at what had just happened.

The bartender, standing behind the bar, yelled out, "Stop

that! There will be no more shooting allowed in here! I got a double-barreled Greener 10 gauge, and I'll use it if you don't holster that weapon!"

Lanie Brooks had stepped around the surprised and disbelieving Larry to take a knee before the downed man. Apparently, everyone believed she was going to the man's aid, no one paid any attention as she snaked a hand inside the man's jacket and retrieved his wallet. She then stood and hurried out the bat wings to disappear in the darkness.

Seconds later, the bat wings swung open as two men rushed through with six-guns extended. The first man, a beefy fellow with a short, red beard and a star on his chest demanded, "Drop that six-gun, fella! You're under arrest!"

The other man, also wearing a badge, stepped behind Larry and stuck the barrel of his six-gun into Larry's kidneys, while the red-bearded man snatched Larry's pistol from the surprised youth's fist.

When Larry twisted to protest, the man behind him slammed the butt of his six-gun to the back of Larry's head. Larry toppled to lie on the floor. A moment later, the officers cuffed his hands behind his back.

The beefy deputy then talked to the bartender and several of the bystander witnesses for a few minutes. No one mentioned Lanie Brooks by name, only that a girl, a soiled dove, was nearby when the shooting happened, but had now disappeared.

Each of the deputies grabbed Larry by a shoulder and dragged him out of the saloon, more or less carrying the youth to the jail, a half-block away.

• • •

Less than an hour later, Marcus and Wayne Creed walked into the saloon in hopes of finding their younger brother still sober. Their intent was to buy Larry a nightcap, then herd him to his hotel room in preparation for tomorrow's departure. Instead, they learned of the shooting and Larry's subsequent arrest. Both men rushed the half-block to the jailhouse across the street.

Inside the building, the red-bearded man, Caleb Ainsworth, newly appointed marshal of Great Bend, sat behind a desk cluttered with papers. "What can I do for you gentlemen?" he asked when the two brothers stepped toward the desk.

Marcus spoke up. "The name is Marcus Creed, and this is my brother, Wayne. We and our hands delivered the T.C. Creed herd to the railroad yesterday. We heard that you have our brother, Larry, locked up for some misunderstanding over at Milt's place, and we're here to see about paying his fine and getting him to his hotel room. We're set to leave in the morning, heading back home to Texas."

Marshall Ainsworth's face suddenly took on sternness. "I don't know who you've been talking to, but the young fella we arrested is charged with more than a little misunderstanding. Witnesses say that he shot and killed a man for no apparent good reason."

"That's crazy, Marshal. Larry wouldn't shoot anyone," Marcus explained. "Why, he's just a kid. Maybe had a little too much to drink, but he's not a killer. Our father, Thomas Creed, will not be happy about this!" he injected, hoping that the mention of his father's name would somehow rectify things.

A half-an-hour later, Thomas Creed, summoned by his two sons, sat before Marshal Ainsworth's desk. The elder Creed was a large man, towering to over six feet tall. He was a rangy man, gray-haired, and his lined face showed he was concerned and upset about what his older sons had told him that had caused Larry to be in jail.

He had just listened as the marshal had reiterated the charges against Larry Creed.

"Are you sure you got the right man?" Creed asked.

Ainsworth's face turned red. "My deputy and I were sitting right here earlier today when a shot rang out. We ran the short distance to where we considered the shot had come from—Milt's Saloon. Inside, we found your son, with a smoking gun in his hand, standing over a fatally wounded man lying on the floor. Yes, I'd say that we got the right man."

"Marshal, I appeal to you to release my son to my custody, and I well see to his punishment of his accused crime. He's not a bad sort—just a kid, in fact—and in need of rightful direction at certain times."

The marshal nodded. "Well, that decision is not up to me, sir. Your son has been charged with killing a man, and now, only a judge can determine his fate."

Thomas Creed grimaced. "Would it be possible to talk to the judge?"

Marshal Ainsworth shook his head. "We do not have a regular judge here in Great Bend. Most likely, a judge in Wichita will handle the case. That's where we'll take your son for trial. I'd say the best thing to do would be for you to get hold of a lawyer to represent the accused when the case is tried."

Thomas Creed nodded his understanding. "Any good lawyers here in Great Bend?"

Ainsworth rolled a shoulder. "I never knew of a good one," he mumbled, obviously having poor thoughts of all lawyers. Then, he said, "There's only one lawyer here in town. Name of Jenkins, William Jenkins. He has an office, first floor over at the Southern Hotel. You most likely won't find him there until about ten tomorrow morning."

• • •

The following morning, Thomas Creed sat in a hard chair before Lawyer Jenkins's desk. A few minutes earlier, Creed had introduced himself, then told of his reason for being here.

"After talking with my son, Larry, and some of the witnesses, it was a bullet from his six-gun that killed the man, all right. But according to Larry, it was unintentional—someone either pushed or nudged his arm at the wrong time and caused the weapon to fire. It was an accident," he explained. Hopefully, he asked, "What do you think?"

Jenkins pursed his lips. "Sounds like a tough one to turn around. Your son caught with a smoking gun in his hand and a man shot dead lying on the floor before him. Open and closed case. The trial most likely won't last long, depending on witness testimony, and it will be up to the judge's discretion to decide his punishment."

Creed nodded. "Well, if he's found guilty, what

alternative does the judge have?"

Jenkins looked at the man soberly. "Judges are the supreme authority. He could sentence the accused to hang, which might take place within days or months. I heard of one such hanging delayed for over ten years. Or, he could dismiss the charges, or simply banish the accused from certain places, such as Great Bend."

"*Banish* you say?" Creed asked with great interest.

Jenkins nodded. "Yes. It's a primitive practice brought over from the old world in an earlier time, but still used in some cases and perfectly legal."

"You seem to be a knowledgeable man, Mr. Jenkins. Will you take the case and see to my son's defense—and hopefully, his release?"

"There are things to take care of first, sir," Jenkins answered, then scribbled on a piece of paper and slid it toward Creed. "I'll need for you to place a retainer before I can begin. Once that's taken care of, I can begin the investigative work—interview your son and the witnesses, so that answers and rebuttals can be presented at the trial."

Creed looked at the amount on the paper and swallowed, then cast his eyes to Jenkins. "Nothing's cheap, I reckon." He then reached a hand into his jacket pocket for his wallet.

Jenkins accepted the cash, then said, "It's going to take a fair amount of time for me to assimilate all the information before we can proceed, and I suppose that you'll most likely go on back to your home in Texas at some point."

"Actually, I'll not be going back until this issue is settled, one way or the other, either to Larry's release or until after the trial. I sent my other two sons and the rest of the herding crew back to the ranch down in Texas this morning." Creed advised. "I'll be nosing around in the meantime…find out all I can about the shooting."

Jenkins nodded. "If you happen to leave town, then I'll need an address where I can reach you in order to keep you informed."

• • •

The next morning, Creed followed Jenkins through the front door when the man opened his office.

Jenkins greeted the man, then stepped behind his desk and held out a hand toward a nearby chair. When Creed had seated himself, Jenkins began. "I interviewed all concerned yesterday except a vital witness, a soiled dove name of Lanie Brooks, who was seen standing right behind Larry at the time of the shooting. Apparently, she and the deceased came to town together. He likely was her pimp. Unfortunately, I have been unable to locate her. I believe she skipped town, possibly not wanting to be further involved.

"If what your son Larry says is true about someone nudging his arm, I believe that she is most likely that person. Even if she did not touch his arm, she would at least be the star witness. If we are to have a chance of winning, I believe that it is imperative for her to testify at the trial. She is likely the only one who heard what the two men said to each other prior to the shooting. What did she see that others did not see—such as, was the victim going for his gun when he was shot? He did have a revolver in his inside suit pocket. What was her relationship to the victim other than him being her pimp? If she was disgruntled with the victim, was it reason enough for her to push your son's arm, causing the weapon to fire?"

"How can we find her?" Creed asked.

Jenkins frowned. "Well, the folks I talked to at Milt's Saloon don't know. Milt says that a number of girls regularly come and go. Some stay a day or so, then drift. Looks like Lanie Brooks, if that is her actual name, left town. Milt said that she and the deceased had been in town previously, possible on a circuit. The marshal cannot say one way or the other, because he doesn't know.

"Mrs. Malcom over at Hotel Malcom, a low-class place, said that Miss Brooks and the deceased had come to town together three days ago. Apparently, Lanie had hurriedly entered the hotel alone right after the shooting, took her things in hand, then left. She then went over to the Star Livery and took the horse and buggy she and the deceased had come to town in and high-tailed it out of town."

"Does the marshal know this?" Creed asked.

Jenkins bobbed his head. "He does, but he will not leave his jurisdiction, which is the city limits of Great Bend, and considers any problems outside the city to be the responsibility of the sheriff of Barton County or federal lawmen."

"What do we do then?" Creed asked.

"Since the evidence is so strong from the other eyewitnesses, I doubt that the sheriff or a federal lawman would see the need to track her down. It might be that the only way to find her would be for you to hire someone to get that done," Jenkins replied.

"Do you have anyone available?"

"I do not have anyone in my employ that could do so. For

one thing, there usually is no need; and for another, the cost to retain said man's service would be prohibitive." He paused for a moment, as if in thought, then said, "I'll have to do some more asking around. Allow me some time—a couple, three hours to do so—then let's meet back here, say at 2:00 p.m. If there is anyone in town capable of tracking, I'll know by then."

Tom wagged his head in frustration. Here he was, chomping at the bit to locate the woman whose testimony might be enough to save his son from the gallows, and it seemed that every way he turned was blocked.

• • •

As soon as Creed had left, Jenkins stepped out of his office and went straight back to Milt's Saloon. He was looking for a man rumored to know of everyone who came to town. He didn't know if he could believe anything the man would offer, but he had no other leads. When he stepped through the batwings, he stood for a moment while looking around the inside of the saloon.

He spotted the man known as "Pops Holmes" sitting at a table in the back side of the room away from the windows. He had the moniker of "Pops" bestowed on him because drinking, funning customers would often ask how old the decrepit-looking man was. Pops always answered by saying he was "sebdy-five."

The saloon owner, Milt, explained, "He doesn't speak good English and he's been saying he is seventy-five ever since I first opened up some six years ago. I'm not sure he even knows how old he is."

Most of the saloon's patrons had it figured that Pops knew everything that went on around town. He would be the one who somehow knew everything about anyone who came to town.

• • •

Wilfred "Pops" Holmes was an obviously elderly man who was in the latter stages of alcoholism and usually only seen drunk. He was potbellied, thin-legged, had a swollen, flushed face and smelled like a privy in bad need of cleaning. He had the stub of a cigarette in one corner of his mouth and was busy rolling another. He had just finished spilling loose tobacco onto a cigarette paper he had cupped, then rolled the newly formed cigarette between his thumb and forefinger and held it up close to lick one edge of the paper. When done, he twisted the ends, then reached to remove the old stub in the corner of his mouth and replace it with the newly formed smoke. He struck a wooden match to life and lit the cigarette.

William Jenkins stepped to the bar to stand in front of Milt, then hooked a thumb toward the back of the room. "What's Pops drinking?" he asked.

Milt raised an eyebrow, then grinned. "Hell, he'll drink anything set before him, but he seems to favor this stuff," he said, as he set an unlabeled bottle on the bar. "It sells for a dollar a bottle. It's the cheapest I have."

The attorney nodded. "I'll take it." He laid a dollar on the bar, grabbed up the bottle, walked over, and set the bottle on the table before the old man. "Mind if I sit, Pops?"

Pops cast an eye to the full bottle, then to the man before him, and merely nodded his head.

Jenkins sat, then said, "I'm looking for someone to do some man tracking. Do you know of anyone around that's any good at it?"

Pops turned to stare at him for a moment, then began talking. Jenkins paid close attention to what the old man said.

• • •

Later that day, Thomas Creed sat before Jenkins's desk and asked the lawyer, "Did you find out anything?"

Jenkins nodded. "I learned of a couple—a man and woman—former bounty hunters, I'm told. They have a place not too far away, over near Hudson, that they occupy. The word around town is that they are retired, but you might talk to them, see if there's any interest."

"Retired, you say? Getting on in years?" T.C. asked while raising an eyebrow.

Jenkins shook his head. "I've never met them, but I did see them ride in one time with a prisoner they were delivering to the jail. I remember that they appeared young—the man in his early thirties, the woman early twenties, I'd say."

CHAPTER TWO

Judd Jacoby was a bounty hunter. He had served in the army during the war. Afterward, with his family's farm destroyed and nothing to go home to, he volunteered to hunt down renegade war offenders. Five years later, when that number had lessened, he cut his ties to the army and drifted into Texas, where he took a job hauling freight.

But a mundane job was not what Judd desired.

He was a medium sized man, an inch less than six feet tall, and weighed 175 pounds, considered a lightweight for bounty hunting by some. He had a lean, angular face, with a strong jaw and pale blue eyes contrasting with his sunburned cheeks. His light brown hair had grown over his ears since his last trim, and his beard of the same color, while not brushy, was a little shabbier than he liked. He dressed conservatively—a chambray shirt and coarse, black cotton pants tucked into knee-high, black flat-heel boots, topped off with a flat-brimmed, flat-topped black hat.

A few years back, a sheriff in Fort Worth had encouraged him to hunt down a man for the three-hundred-dollar bounty on the criminal's head. It took a month of hard riding before he brought the man in and established himself as a bounty hunter. He figured at that time that he would only pursue wanted men if the bounty was at least five hundred dollars, having learned that chasing men for lesser fees took the same amount of time and effort. Those larger bounties were reserved for the more hardened thieves and murderers, scoundrels of all sorts.

Tracking wanted men required patience, single-minded concentration, and the willingness to kill, if necessary. Judd was no gunslinger, even though those he hunted usually were. But he could be accurate with his six-gun when he needed to be, and he was willing—and that combination usually counted for more than speed of the draw and shoot. He held no fear of those he hunted; after all, they were no different from the war criminals he had tangled with. The mid-west and southwest portions of the country were the outlaws' homeland, lots of open space, little law enforcement and plenty of places to hide.

Judd had cashed in on several wanted men he brought in. Then, he learned of a pair of bank robbers with sizable bounties offered on them. A shot by one of the men during the holdup hit a customer and killed him. Judd tracked the two, identified as Joaquin Higgins and Lonnie Sims to their nighttime camp. At first light the next day, he called for their surrender. A bullet within three inches of his head was the reply.

In the early morning shootout that followed, Higgins took a bullet that put him down for good. Sims also took a bullet from Judd's six-gun. The bullet to Sims's shoulder had put the young man down but it was not a fatal shot. Judd was able to capture Sims without further gunfire and took possession of the remainder of the stolen loot from the bank. He doused Sims's wound with whiskey from a nearby half-full bottle despite the young man's howling, then bound a strip of a shirt from Higgins's saddle bag around Sims's upper body.

He then loaded the body of Joaquin Higgins onto Higgins's horse and tied the horse's reins to the tail of Lonnie Sims's horse. Judd had shackled Lonnie Sims's hands in front, then put him on his horse and tied the man's hands to his saddle horn. He then led the procession toward Hays City, Kansas, where there was a jail.

He had traveled until the sun on the horizon began to fade. He happened onto the camp of Jonas and Maggie McJunkin, along with their somewhat wild eighteen-year-old daughter, Faye.

After explaining who he was and what he was doing, the McJunkins invited him to share their camp. A little later, he learned that Jonas and Maggie were returning their runaway wayward daughter to their home. Judd untied Sims from his horse, and then shackled him to a hardwood sapling at the edge of the camp. He then unloaded the body of Higgins and laid it out in an area distant from the McJunkins' campfire, but close to where he had laid his bedroll.

Later on, while Judd was caring for the horses, Faye struck up a conversation with Lonnie Sims. The desperate prisoner promised Faye the moon and a good time if she would only help him escape. When Judd saw the two talking, he admonished Faye and demanded that she keep her distance from his prisoner, followed by her mother's likewise instructions.

Late that night, while her parents and Judd slept, Faye quietly sneaked to Judd's side with a rock in hand. She smashed it to Judd's head twice to make sure he was out. She then took the keys to Sims's shackles and released the excited youth. The two then took the saddlebags with the loot and all of Judd's weapons. They saddled and mounted Judd's and Lonnie Sims's horses. They also led Joaquin's horse on a lead rope when they left, leaving Judd without a means to pursue them.

Judd awoke the next morning under the concerned and careful ministrations of Maggie placing a cool cloth to his aching head. She attempted to apologize for Faye's actions. Judd knew it was not the fault of the parents because their daughter had become wild, misguided, and out of control.

"She's only creating problems for herself," Judd assured them.

Judd discovered that not only were Faye and Sims missing, but so was the bank loot, along with all the horses, as well. They had also taken Judd's six-gun and Winchester rifle, leaving him unconscious, unarmed, and afoot.

Judd was beside himself, left adrift and powerless to defend himself, he could not object when Jonas and Maggie offered to take Judd and the body of Joaquin Higgins to Hays City in their wagon. It took three days for the plodding mules to make the trip.

When they arrived in Hays City, Judd had Jonas stop the wagon in front of the county sheriff's office. Sheriff Dean Ellis and Judd took the aromatic body of Higgins from the wagon for identification. Ellis confirmed the identity, which allowed Judd to receive a portion of the promised reward from the bank, until the actual reward arrived. He could then purchase, guns, a horse, and trail supplies in order to begin a pursuit of Sims and Faye.

Judd bought a fine-looking horse, a line back dun, along with a used saddle and bridle. He also purchased a .45 Colt six-gun, gun belt and holster, and a sixteen shot Henry rifle. He also bought a coffee pot, a skillet, and enough trail supplies to last for a week's worth of travel.

Judd spent the night in town, then left at first light the following morning, heading in a northern direction. He figured that was the route Lonnie Sims and Faye had headed.

• • •

Three days later, Judd had an early morning breakfast in his camp, then saddled his horse and mounted up. With no trail to follow, Judd cut across country. An hour later, he smelled the smoke of a nearby camp. He had no intention of intruding, but then he heard the distressed cry of a woman, which caused him to duck his head in a move to remain hidden.

There was a faint movement down in a ravine some forty or fifty yards away. He studied the area, then clearly heard a woman plead, "Please, let me go! I won't say a word."

It sounded as if the woman was in trouble. It wasn't *his* trouble, but his grandmother's words of, "Always try to do the right thing, Judd, and let the Lord lead you," plus his own past of hunting down criminals, prevented him from riding away without knowing what the problem was.

The woman begged again, "Please, let me go."

A man's gruff voice replied, "Shut up your whining and

get me some coffee!"

Judd slipped from his saddle, tied the reins to a spindly oak bush, palmed his six-gun, and started down the brushy ravine. When he was within twenty feet of the camp, he crouched to ground level and peered through the brush. Judd was surprised to recognize that Faye McJunkin was the one doing the pleading to be let go. She wore the same flimsy dress she had on back in her parents' camp. The dress, however, was now just a torn, filthy rag hanging from her shoulders.

Off to her left were two slovenly men. Both men wore well-used and filthy cotton shirts, denim pants, and scarred boots. Each man had a six-gun in a well-used holster belted to his middle. One man seated on a log had his back to Judd, the other man stood towering over Faye. "Get up and get busy!" he demanded. Faye merely bawled loudly.

Judd stood, extended his six-gun, then stepped forward. Neither of the men had seen him yet when he spoke up. "I believe the lady is tired of your company," he announced. "She'll be leaving with me."

The surprised man turned to face Judd. "Who the hell are you?"

Judd stood, steely-eyed. "Her benefactor."

The man now standing beside the log he had been sitting on yelled, "The hell!" He jabbed a hand toward his six-gun.

With his six-gun pointed at the man's middle, Judd pulled the trigger of the .45. The pistol barked, and Judd watched as the man fell backward onto the campfire.

The other man standing nearby then smoothly drew his six-gun and fired it toward Judd. The bullet missed Judd by a hair as Judd fired his own weapon at the man. Judd's bullet hit the man in the chest, causing the outlaw to trigger his six-gun again.

Unfortunately, the six-gun was still pointing in Judd's direction. It was a wild shot that sent a bullet to crease the right side of Judd's head, putting the bounty hunter down and out.

When Judd awakened to sunlight and a throbbing headache, he quickly learned from Faye McJunkin that he had been out for three days. He was mystified that the very woman who had knocked him out and seen to Sims's escape had now been seeing to his care for three days.

When he asked, Faye replied, "I just felt the need to try to do something good and try to right the wrong I've done to you."

Judd nodded. "You saved my life, and I'm grateful for that."

He then asked, "What about those two that I shot?"

Faye shrugged a shoulder. "They found me wandering along the morning after Lonnie had left me. They weren't interested in my problems of being left stranded, only what I could do for them—which was to cook, clean, and lay with each of them. You have no idea how grateful I am that you came along when you did, Judd, and stopped them. I do not doubt that they would have killed me after they tired of using me.

"After you appeared to be resting okay, I took one of the horses and dragged them to a ravine." She pointed to her right. "Saw no need to bury trash," she quipped.

Judd could not argue with that.

When she noticed Judd staring at the shirt she was wearing, she said, "I helped myself to a shirt and pants you had in your saddlebags. Hope you don't mind. My dress was in tatters."

She then noted, "I went through their things. I kept the money, eighteen dollars they had between them, and I figure they owed it to me for services rendered. I also set aside their six-guns and rifles, figure to keep the one .44 and Winchester rifle, which I know how to use, and sell the other ones. I plan to keep the paint horse and saddle and sell the other one."

Judd spent another night resting under Faye's watchful eyes. The next morning, he was feeling much better and told Faye that it was time for him to get onto Sims's trail. "You said that Lonnie told you that he was going to Ogallala to meet up with some friends," Judd said. "I figure to ride up there and nose around a bit."

Faye wanted to catch up to Sims, the rat who had abandoned her, as much as Judd did.

"I'll be going along with you, Judd."

Judd stared at her but did not reply.

• • •

It took the pair five days of riding to reach Ogallala. Their first stop was at the sheriff's office, and they met with Sheriff Ron Flagg. It didn't take long for Judd to tell the sheriff who they were and that they had come to town in search of Lonnie Sims, then gave a description of Sims's physical features.

The sheriff nodded. "I'm not familiar with the name; however, that description fits one of four men who just this past week robbed, beat, and left for dead cattle buyer Stanton

Lilly. They got twenty thousand dollars of Mr. Lilly's money. Mr. Lilly is offering a $2500.00 reward for each of the culprits. I might add that two other bounty hunters are on their trail as we speak."

Judd was ready to get on the robber's trail until Faye spoke up. "It would be best if you saw a doctor before we head out again."

Judd, knowing she was right, nodded. "Well, let's go see what he has to say."

• • •

Two hours later, Doctor Theodore Rasmussen gave him an examination and questioned him at length. The doctor's prognosis was simple. "You need rest—and plenty of it—to let the body heal itself." Because his knowledge of the brain was limited, he explained, he recommended that Judd see a known brain specialist in St. Louis, Doctor Emil Torgerson.

Immediately after visiting Doctor Rasmussen, Judd and Faye left town and headed south. Three days later, they came upon the camp of Belton Matlock and Ron Kelp, the two other bounty hunters who had taken up the trail of the four robbers. The bounty men had two of the culprits in custody. One man was dead; the other badly injured with a stomach wound, and not expected to survive much longer.

Matlock suggested that Judd and Faye continue the chase for the two other robbers, Lonnie Sims and Red Bonner, as he and Kelp were heading to Ellsworth, a two-day ride, to redeem the two they had captured for the bounty. "They might not be too far away," Kelp said. "I think Ron wounded one of them—I believe it was Bonner. I saw him lurch in the saddle as they rode away."

Judd picked up the escaping men's trail, and two hours later found badly wounded Red Bonner at an isolated roadhouse. Judd, after an explanation of who he was and who the wounded man was, purchased a well-used buckboard from the relieved roadhouse owner. Judd and Faye loaded Bonner, wrapped in a blanket, into the bed of the wagon, and drove straight to the Ellsworth sheriff's office where Judd turned the thief in to claim the bounty on the man.

Afterward, Judd and Faye drove to a nearby livery. Faye busied herself with the livery owner in an attempt to sell the now unneeded wagon and team to him while Judd wandered around and discovered his own stolen horse in the livery's corral.

When asked about the rider, the livery owner said, "Young fella, didn't give a name, already paid me, and said he'd be leaving early tomorrow."

On the way to the hotel, Judd had suffered a dizzy spell and became unsteady on his feet. Faye took his arm and guided him to the hotel. Faye checked them in, then accompanied Judd to a second-story room. Once inside, Judd went right to bed, and was asleep in moments.

• • •

Early the next morning while Judd was still asleep, Faye had left the room with the intent to waylay Sims at the livery when he came to get his horse. Just after dawn, Sims entered the livery, led the horse out of the stall and busied himself saddling the animal.

That was when Faye called out, "Don't move! I've got you

covered!"

Sims recognized the woman's voice and attempted to smooth talk her, but Faye would have none of it. Sims, with no options left, threw a lantern at Faye and followed it to overpower her, pushing her to the ground. Faye was able to get off one shot, which hit Sims in the calf muscle of his left leg.

Sims rolled to his side, then palmed his six-gun. He was ready to shoot Faye when Judd called out from the doorway, "Drop it, Sims, or I'll fire." Sims reacted by firing a shot at Judd, who ducked the shot and returned the fire. Judd's shot hit Sims in his upper right arm, causing Sims to drop his six-gun and fall to the ground where he had been crouching.

Judd rushed forward and cuffed the writhing young man. He and Faye tied bandanas around Sims's wounds, then escorted him to jail. Once there, since he already had the reward on Bonner coming to him, Judd informed the deputy to put the reward due on Sims in Faye's name. He had done that in appreciation for all the help that Faye had given him. She'd cared for him and saving his life after he'd received the head wound while rescuing her from her abductors, and she'd stuck with him and looked out for him since that time.

Though he had attempted to get her to leave his side and go about her life several times previously, she'd declined. He now believed that perhaps with the $2500.00 reward money on Sims that she was to receive, she could begin a new life somewhere out of danger.

Faye apparently had different ideas; she left instructions for the deputy to deposit the money in her name at the local bank.

• • •

The next morning, while Judd and Faye were having breakfast, Deputy Jeff Carson stopped by their table. "Just wanted to let you know that your reward money will be here by noon today."

Carson then told of two men who robbed a bank and horse-trampled a woman in the street in Great Bend, just a day ago. Judd knew that Great Bend was about forty miles southwest of Ellsworth.

Judd was itching to get on the road after the culprits, but Faye interjected. "I have tickets for the train to St. Louis for you to see Doctor Torgerson. I already made the appointment."

Judd was greatly surprised. "When did you do that?"

"If you must know, I made the arrangements when you were sleeping yesterday," Faye had replied.

After enduring jostling train rides for two days, they'd finally arrived in St. Louis. The next day, Faye went with Judd to his appointed time with Doctor Torgerson. Judd was disappointed to learn that the good doctor's advice was the same as Doctor Rasmussen. "Rest, and plenty of it," both doctors had said.

Judd was eager to get back to Ellsworth. He wanted to outfit himself and get on the trail of the Great Bend bank robbers. He insisted that they catch the 6:00 p.m. train to Kansas City. They arrived at 2:00 a.m., then spent the rest of the night at a hotel. Mid-morning, they caught a coach that arrived in Ellsworth late in the afternoon, where they spent the night.

• • •

The next morning at the sheriff's office, Judd had learned from Deputy Deg Watson that there were rewards offered on the Great Bend bank robbers: five hundred offered by the trampled and now-dead woman's husband, and another five hundred offered by the bank for the return of the stolen three thousand dollars. Watson also told Judd that two men matching the robbers' descriptions had eaten a meal at the home of a farmer named Walls and his daughter near a community named Hudson, some fifteen miles from Great Bend, near the Walnut River.

Judd and Faye had ridden to Hudson to speak with self-proclaimed town marshal Gunter Hinds. Upon arrival, they talked briefly with Hinds and got directions to Elmer Walls's farm where the two suspected bank robbers had dined.

When the two rode into the yard, Walls's daughter, Evelyn Ramstad, had greeted them and invited them for tea. Faye and Evelyn hit it off immediately, gabbing and smiling, while Elmer Walls was a little indifferent to bounty hunters in general.

Judd and Faye had learned that the suspects had, indeed, had a meal there, leaving a five-dollar tip and, knowingly or not, had disclosed their first names, Rudy and Clarence. Judd and Faye, at the insistence of Evelyn Ramstad, had spent the night. It was then that Evelyn had recommended that the two give up bounty hunting, settle down, and raise a family. "There's a place bordering our property, the Holgorsen place, which happens to be for sale," she had said, seemingly enthusiastic to that end.

The next morning, after leaving the Walls's farm, Judd and Faye had spent all day riding in circles, following old tracks that led across the Walnut River. They made a camp, and the next morning, they resumed following what tracks they believed were Rudy's and Clarence's horse tracks, which was a meandering northeastern course that seemed to head toward Ellsworth. They rode until mid-morning when they spotted the Crossroads Inn, a roadhouse situated in a small valley. The two had pulled up in front, dismounted, then tied their reins to the hitching rail.

Inside, Judd and Faye both immediately recognized a man matching the description of Clarence seated at a nearby table. Judd and Faye had each ordered breakfast. They attempted to act inconspicuous while noting Clarence sitting quietly, but his posture had stiffened since their arrival. When Judd asked the server if many folks stopped by here on their way to Ellsworth, he noticed that Clarence stood up.

Judd figured that he would not waste this opportunity to confront the man, so he asked, "That you, Clarence?"

Before Clarence could answer, Judd had his six-gun pointed at the man, who slowly raised his hands. Judd stepped to disarm Clarence and placed him in shackles. At the same time, Faye, having heard voices in a nearby room, hurried there, and had brother Rudy at gunpoint.

After breakfast, Judd and Faye, along with their two manacled prisoners, had ridden the thirty miles to Ellsworth and delivered the Grider brothers and the balance of the bank loot, less about $500.00 the brothers had blown, to the sheriff's office.

At that time, they learned from the deputy that two

known thieves held up the one bank in town. They immediately got on the trail of Carl Sturgis and Dan Perkins. Judd and Faye trailed the culprits to a homestead cabin belonging to Jacob Eldridge, located some two hours' ride south of Ellsworth. They knew that Dan Perkins had received a bullet wound in a saloon shootout, and the two men on the run had most likely taken refuge in the cabin to see to Perkins's wound.

By observation, from a distance, Judd saw that a dog guarded the place, and he was certain the dog would alert others of any intruder. He also witnessed a woman in the cabin's doorway talking to two mounted men who had just ridden in. Judd figured that woman was caring for the wounded Perkins, and that one of the mounted men was the cabin's owner, but the other matched the description of Carl Sturgis. Later, when it was very dark out, Sturgis and the owner retired to the barn, apparently to sleep there, leaving the cabin for the woman to care for Perkins.

Judd and Faye had cooked up a plan, as a distraction, for Faye to ride into the yard later and proclaim that she was a traveler and needed help for her husband who was a victim of an accident.

A few hours later, when it was full dark out, Sturgis had emerged from the barn and busied himself saddling his horse in the adjoining corral. The man had it in mind to leave the place secretly, abandoning his grievously wounded partner Perkins to the care of others. At the same time, Faye rode into the yard and began her story of needing help. The dog, a spotted mongrel, had begun barking and growling at the strange horse and rider.

Judd had stuck to the shadows as he crept forward, then called out to Sturgis to give up. The reply was in the form of a bullet just over Judd's head. He returned the fire and heard a grunt, then saw the flash of a six-gun as Sturgis sent another bullet toward the mounted Faye.

The bullet hit Faye's horse in the head between the animal's eyes, killing it instantly. Before Faye could jump free, the animal fell to its side and onto Faye's right leg, breaking the upper leg bone in two places above the right knee. Other than an immediate groan, Faye had remained silent when the horse fell on top of her.

Judd knew his bullet had hit Sturgis but was more concerned about Faye. He rushed to her side. She was awake, but obviously in pain. Judd said, "Hold on, I'll get that horse off of you in just a minute."

He then ran to find Sturgis lying on the ground, writhing from having suffered a bullet wound to his lower left side. The bullet had gone completely through the man, exiting his back. The force of the bullet was enough to put the man unconscious and out of commission. Judd picked up Sturgis's six-gun, which lay where the man had dropped it.

After identifying himself and Faye to Jacob Eldridge, the property owner, Eldridge helped Judd get Faye from under the horse and moved her into the cabin where the woman inside began seeing to Faye's mangled leg. Judd and Eldridge then carried the comatose Sturgis into the cabin, as well.

Two days later, after learning that Perkins had died, Judd needed to take the body to Ellsworth for identification in order to collect the bounty on the dead man, as well as turning in the wounded Sturgis.

Though the woman had carefully set Faye's broken leg and it appeared straight, he also wanted to get a doctor to look at her broken limb to make sure it would heal correctly.

Judd had tied Perkins's body to one of the outlaw's horses, tied the reins to his own horse's tail, then mounted his horse. Judd followed behind a wagon driven by Jacob Eldridge, seated next to Maria Cortez, who had been caring for Perkins and Sturgis as well as Faye. In the bed of the wagon, the wounded and quiet Sturgis lay bundled on one side while Faye lay in blankets on the other side.

They arrived in town late that afternoon. Judd checked Faye, Maria Cortez, Jacob Eldridge, and himself into the Garland Hotel. He had the desk clerk summon Doctor Wilson to see to Faye, then he and Jacob took Sturgis and Perkins to the jail where Judd put in claims for the bounty offered on both men.

Afterward, Judd talked to Doctor Wilson, who commended Maria Cortez for setting Faye's broken leg correctly.

Doctor Wilson then said, "I went ahead and put a cast on the leg. It would be best if she stayed off of it for a few weeks and give it a chance to heal properly."

• • •

Three days later after, saying their goodbyes to Jacob Eldridge and Maria Cortez, Judd and Faye sat having their early morning breakfast when Deputy Jeff Carson walked up to their table.

"Morning, Faye...Judd," he offered. He then told them their reward money would arrive either today or tomorrow.

He also informed them of bounties offered on two men who had held up the stage from Dodge City to Great Bend. They had shot and wounded a man who was carrying an undisclosed amount of cash, from the sale of a ranch, in a satchel.

Judd thanked the man for the information then pointed to Faye's cast enclosed leg stretched out before the table and said, "We might sit this one out while Faye heals up."

After the deputy left, Faye asked, "Are you saying that you would forsake going after a bounty because I'm laid up, Judd?"

Judd was quick to answer. "That, and other things." He not only felt obligated to see to the woman's recovery, but to his own recovery from those cursed dizzy spells, as well.

He explained, "We've been at it rather hard lately. It's time for you to take it easy for a while. The doctor said you'll have that cast on for six to eight weeks, and when he does take it off, you'll still need to limit your activities for some months afterward before you can do any lengthy horseback riding and such.

"When you're up to it, I thought we might take a carriage and go take a look at that property over near Hudson that Evelyn Ramstad mentioned was for sale. With the rewards coming, we can both afford it." He didn't look at her directly, because he didn't want to give her any false hope about their becoming a couple.

But when he did cast a gaze in her direction, the hope was there, and it made him confused and uncomfortable. She was the reason he was alive in the first place, and he knew that she had fallen in love with him. He was not in love with her—at least, he didn't think he was—but he had grown accustomed to her being near, and that gave him comfort.

He was not asking her to marry him; he wasn't ready to make that commitment. He thought that, given time, he might learn to trust her; he could love her as well, and they could maybe find happiness together at some time down the trail. However, they had a ways to go, time to pass before he could start thinking about such things as settling down.

Despite all the care she had given him, he was still somewhat wary because of her actions of braining him at their first meeting. He wondered if, at some point, she would turn on him again.

What he had in mind for the present was to get her into some place where they both could heal up. If that meant putting aside bounty hunting and purchasing property together—each of them paying half—so be it.

• • •

Faye, though unsure of Judd's intentions, was flabbergasted. She was not totally convinced that Judd had forgiven her for having run off with the cad, Lonnie Sims, and leaving Judd defenseless. Nevertheless, when Judd had rescued her from the clutches of those two scoundrels a few days later and was wounded doing so, she had devoted herself to seeing to his care.

Was Judd now saying he would be willing for them to purchase a place for the two of them to call home? She wondered. Was he asking for her hand in marriage after he had spurned any affection she had previously attempted to give him? All she knew was that it sounded too good to be true. She answered simply by saying, "I'd love to see the place, and I'll be ready to go whenever you are, Judd."

Judd gave her a smile. "I know your leg is hurting badly right now. I want you to rest up for a day or so before we venture over there to see if the place is still available. That'll give me time to line up a carriage for the trip."

CHAPTER THREE

Two days later, Judd helped Faye into the carriage he had rented. He kept the livery mare, an energetic big-boned bay, at a steady but easy pace for the 30-mile trip, arriving at the familiar Walls farm by mid-afternoon.

It seemed to Judd as if two long-lost relatives were meeting when Evelyn Ramstad rushed from the house, then climbed into the carriage and hugged Faye. The two began gabbing like schoolchildren. Elmer Walls stepped out of the house to stand solemnly nearby.

When Judd finally had an opportunity to speak to the women, he said, "We just wanted to get directions to that property Evelyn said was for sale. If it's still available, we'll drive over, talk to the owner, and take a look before it gets dark, then be on our way."

Evelyn Ramstad shook her head. "Nonsense. Faye's already had a long day in that carriage and needs some care. If you'll help her down, we can get her into the house. Faye already told me that you were in no hurry, so you can spend the night. That will allow plenty of time for you two to go talk with Emma Holgerson tomorrow. In the meantime, I'll see to Faye, and Father will help you see to your mare and the carriage."

Elmer Walls stepped forward and said, "There's oats and hay in the barn. I'll bring some out to that manger by the wall." He pointed to the manger to the right of the barn's double doors.

Judd nodded then unhooked the mare from the carriage and led her over to a watering trough, then slipped the bit from her mouth so the horse could drink freely. When she had finished drawing water, the mare raised her head. Judd led her over to the manger and took a scrap of burlap, offered by Elmer, and began to wipe the animal down as the hungry mare began to munch the oats.

Judd spoke as he rubbed the mare. "As you no doubt noticed, Faye had a bit of bad luck; her horse fell on top of her leg and broke it." He saw no need to explain the details of Faye's injury or his own troubling dizzy spells to the man. He then said, "Most hotel rooms are on the second or third floor, and that makes it difficult to care for someone who can't get around very well. So, we decided to go looking for a worthwhile place, to possibly buy, so we can sit tight for a while and allow her to heal."

Elmer Walls, though at odds at Judd's profession at the last visit, seemed pleased when Judd told him of his and Faye's intentions. "I know that Emma will be glad that someone has taken an interest in purchasing her place; fact is, she's been worried that she'd just have to abandon the property. I personally would hate to see that happen. Some riffraff might move in and bring all kinds of trouble along with them. You, being used to handling such, would surely be a plus for the area. I figure you'd make a good neighbor, Judd. I can tell you all about the place while those two women in there are talking things out. Evelyn gets lonely for conversation with someone other than me. Not very many women folk out here, and we don't get to town very often," he explained.

The man did not wait for a response from Judd; he immediately went into a story. "When Congress passed the Homestead Act back in 1862, it allowed anyone paying the $14.00 filing fee to homestead one hundred and sixty acres and call it his own. I was one of the first in line to file on this property, nigh on to twenty years ago. Ole Jacob and Emma Holgerson filed a homestead on their place some twelve years ago. One hundred and sixty pretty good acres.

"First thing he did was to dig a well; hit good water at twenty feet. I helped Jacob build the house, which includes a kitchen, living room, and two rooms for bedding or storage. Later on, he built a small barn and a roomy corral. Before he died, he raised some beef cattle over there, did quite well at it, according to Emma.

"Since Jacob's passing, Emma hasn't had either the knowhow or the desire to continue herding and caring for the animals, so she sold off all the livestock, excepting a milk cow and his and her saddle horses. Wants to keep both the horses for some reason; pets, I suppose, but said that the milk cow would go with the property."

Before Elmer could continue, Judd said, "Sounds like Mrs. Holgerson's place would fit what me and Faye I are interested in." Then he asked, "Do you know how much she is asking for the property?"

Elmer grimaced and wrinkled his forehead. "As far as I know, she's asking $2200.00 for everything. Which includes the land, house, and all the furnishings. The furnishings would be a woodstove for heat, cook stove for cooking, a double bed, dresser, couch, dining room table and chairs, a few lamps and such. Then there's the barn, the well, and all of Jacob's working and farming tools. She told me that she just wants to take her clothes and the two horses and leave everything else that is there for the new owners."

Judd nodded his understanding. Without looking at the place, he had already checked on prices with a real estate agent back in Ellsworth. Land was going for anywhere from $5.00 to $8.00 an acre, a 4-room house would cost around $500 to $700.00 to build, a barn $75.00; an existing well was worth another $75.00. Added together, there was at least $2000.00 value there. The woman's asking price of $2200.00 did not seem to be out of line.

Elmer saw fit to add, "I'd like to see Emma get a price close to what she's asking. She's going to need every nickel she can get to re-establish herself elsewhere." He shrugged a shoulder. "Course, any asking price is negotiable." He gave Judd a nod. "Evelyn and I would be happy to ride over tomorrow and introduce you to Emma."

• • •

The next day after a bountiful breakfast of bacon, eggs, flapjacks, and coffee provided by the constantly chattering Evelyn Ramstad, Elmer and Judd retreated to the barn to ready their respective horses and carriages for the short trip to the Holgerson place.

Emma Holgerson stood on the front porch to watch as the two carriages pulled into the front yard. After Evelyn made the introductions and gave a smiling approval of the new prospects to the delighted Emma Holgerson, she and Elmer turned their carriage around and left.

Both Faye and Judd declined the offer of coffee, opting to get to looking the place over. Faye hobbled around inside the house, with Judd's assistance, as Emma pointed out each room and its contents. Later, she told Judd of the boundaries. He stepped outside leaving the women to gab. Judd walked the circumference of the nearby homestead grounds, noting the landmarks the woman had pointed out, then toured the outbuildings, barn, privy, and a tool shed.

A little past the noon hour, and at Emma's insistence, they enjoyed a filling meal of a stew and some fluffy biscuits she had cooked. Afterward, while sipping coffee, Judd began the negotiations.

An hour later, he and Faye agreed to purchase the property, the house, and the contents for $2100.00. "We'll be back in two days with a bank draft, Mrs. Holgerson. Or, if you prefer, we'll pay you in cash," Judd informed her.

The woman smiled. "Why don't you spend the night, then in the morning, since I am only taking my clothes and my two horses, what do you think about me accompanying you to town? That way, we can do our business, and right after I can be on my way while you folks can return when you're ready."

Judd looked at Faye. She smiled broadly then nodded in approval.

"That would be fine, Emma," Judd said. "You can ride

with Faye in the carriage, and I'll follow along leading your horses. We can stop by and tell Elmer and Evelyn of our decisions on our way to town."

• • •

They arrived in Ellsworth by mid-afternoon. At the insistence of both women, they went straight to the bank and conducted the transfer of funds. Emma Holgerson preferred cash, so Faye counted out $1050.00, and Judd did the same. A bank clerk issued a receipt to them, and the deal was completed. Judd then made sure both women had hotel rooms, then he returned the carriage and Emma's two horses to the livery before he retreated to his own hotel room.

The next day, Emma, with her two horses loaded into a boxcar, left town on a train headed north.

Judd and Faye stayed in town an extra day to rest up, then the next day, the two drove the carriage, loaded down with supplies they had purchased, into the yard of their new property. Judd had his horse tethered to the back of the carriage. Since they were getting plenty of use of the carriage, Judd went ahead and bought it from the livery owner along with a paint mare that Faye picked out to pull it and most likely use as a riding mount later on.

They'd settled into the house and had a supper of fried chicken, potatoes, and biscuits that Judd had purchased in town before they'd headed home. Judd, having cared for the animals, was tired from all the day's activities and retired to his bedroom early.

When he awakened to sun-filled windows, he noticed that Faye sat in a chair near his bed. Judd wondered why she was sitting in his bedroom. He was startled when Faye said, "Well, glad to see you are still with us, Judd."

"What time is it?" he asked. "I overslept."

Faye stared at him. "You've been sleeping for a day and a half, Judd. It is now Wednesday. I knew you were tired when you went to bed Monday night, what with everything that was going on. Us buying the property, getting settled in, and you having to care for me as well as the animals were reason enough for you to rest for an extended time. In addition, it just confirms Doctor Torgerson's diagnosis—you need to rest and take it easy for your own good. I'm sorry for what I did to you back in my parents' camp…that caused all this to happen. I wasn't thinking straight, but things are different now. Rest assured I am here to help you in any way I can."

Judd sat up. "I feel okay, now. Soon as I get some coffee down me, I'll need to go see to the horses and milk that cow."

Faye nodded. "I'll have breakfast ready by the time you get your chores done."

Before he could give a rebuttal, Faye said, "I'm not totally an invalid, Judd. I have a cane, and I have chores to do, as well."

• • •

By nightfall, both Judd and Faye were fatigued and ready to stop for the day, though neither had done anything that would work up a sweat.

When Judd went into his bedroom and had undressed, he lay down. Faye clumped into the room. He watched as she began undressing, all the while silently staring at him, perhaps to see if he would spurn her again. Judd said nothing and didn't argue when she slid into bed next to him and pressed her body next to his. His arousal was immediate. He had not had relations with a woman for a long time and she had not been with a man almost as long.

Ever since their second meeting, he had shunned her affections for fear of a lack of sincerity, but now that all seemed like history. Either that, or he just no longer cared about their past. All he knew was that he was a man with natural wants and needs and she was a young woman with those same feelings. Now was the right time to engage in satisfying the lust they had been holding back, and they did so eagerly, exploring one another's body before fulfilling their needs. They spent the rest of the night cuddling each other and eventually sleeping.

The next day, Judd vacated his things from the now spare room and moved into her bedroom—theirs, now.

• • •

For the next few weeks, Faye remained in the house while Judd puttered doing endless maintenance chores around the place. They sat at the dinner table each night and chatted about the day's events. The prospect of marriage never came up, although the couple acted and appeared as such.

Judd was feeling well—rested, in fact—and had not had another bout of dizziness or sleeping for an extended time.

Faye felt that she had healed and wanted desperately to get the cast off her leg.

Judd insisted that they travel to Ellsworth, let the doctor have a look, and hopefully, he would remove the cumbersome cast.

The next day, exactly two months to the day that Faye's leg was broken, they made the trip, and were delighted when Doctor Wilson proclaimed, "Yes, it is time to remove the cast," and he proceeded to do so. "Be extra careful and watchful so that you do nothing to reinjure yourself. In particular, if I were you, I'd refrain from riding a horse," he advised.

CHAPTER FOUR

Four months later, Judd, standing in the barn doorway, saw a lone rider headed toward the house. He immediately stepped inside and took hold of the Henry rifle he kept within easy reach. He never knew when some disgruntled former captive or relative of such was now out for revenge.

The only visitors he and Faye had seen since moving in were their immediate neighbors, Evelyn and Elmer. Judd stayed in the barn's doorway, with the Henry held loosely, as the man rode to within a dozen feet of Judd.

"Good morning, sir. I'm T.C. Creed from southern Texas. Are you Judd Jacoby?" the man asked.

Mr. Creed's demeanor did not appear aggressive, so Judd, now curious as to the visit, nodded. "Yes, what is it that you need help with, Mister Creed?"

"I'm looking for a young woman, a soiled dove by the name of Lanie Brooks. The law enforcement in Great Bend told me that you might be able to help me locate her. She was witness to—possibly played a part—in a shooting involving my son. He admits to having shot a man, but not on purpose. The law in Great Bend arrested him right after the shooting.

Now, we're awaiting the arrival of a judge to Wichita where the trial is to take place."

Judd, intrigued by why the man figured that he could help, extended a hand. "Step down. Let your horse water while you tell me about it."

T.C. dismounted, then led his horse to the water tank fronting the barn. He slipped the bit from the horse's mouth so that the animal could drink with ease, then turned to face Judd.

"Not much to it," he began. "Three nights ago, my son, Larry, and the other Creed drovers were in Milt's Saloon, there in Great Bend. They were all doing their celebrating for having finished delivering the Creed Ranch herd to the stock pens. I wasn't present, but as I understand it, things got out of hand when the girl's male companion—most likely her pimp—tried to take her away from my son's table.

"Apparently, Larry didn't like the man's manner and pulled his six-gun on him. Unfortunately—and unintentionally—it discharged, sending a bullet to the man's chest, which killed him."

He paused for a moment. "I have to explain that Larry is only nineteen years old and pretty mild-mannered. Prior to this incident, he has never shot anyone, or even shot *at* anyone that I am aware of. He wore the pistol, I believe, because he wanted to fit in with his fellow cattle drovers who usually have a six-shooter strapped on their side. He told me that he pulled the six-gun for show, hoping the pimp would go away.

"Unfortunately, he had cocked the weapon. Someone— he believes this girl, Lanie Brooks—pushed his arm hard enough that the six-gun discharged. There is no doubt that the bullet from Larry's six-gun killed the man, but Larry adamantly proclaims that it was unintentional.

"To complicate matters, this Lanie Brooks left town that night, right after the incident, and no one knows where she went to or where she came from. It is imperative that I locate her and bring her back to testify at Larry's trial; otherwise, based on the evidence from the other witnesses, the judge is apt to sentence Larry to hang."

Judd had listened with interest as T.C. had explained what his problem was. "Were you told that I'm a bounty hunter?" Judd asked. "I usually hunt down dangerous men with a price on their head. I've actually been out of circulation for a little over four months and have no prospects for returning to the profession any time soon. Are you seriously asking me to locate a soiled dove and bring her to Great Bend? It sounds to me like you're in need of a snoop detective rather than a gun for hire."

Creed nodded. "I was told by others that you're an accomplished bounty hunter—a man used to going after criminals and bringing them to justice. I figured I'd see if I could interest you in hunting this woman down. She may not be willing to return to Great Bend, given the circumstance."

He paused, then said, "Time is of the essence, Mister Jacoby, and there is no one else, that I'm aware of, available in Great Bend. I'm willing to pay a bounty for you to locate and deliver Lanie Brooks to Wichita, whether she is willing to accompany you or not. I'm willing to pay you five thousand dollars to do so; a thousand dollars up front and an additional four thousand dollars upon your delivery of the woman to Wichita in time to testify at the trial. I will put the money on deposit at the bank, here in town."

Judd was amazed, though skeptical; the likelihood of locating a particular soiled dove, whose name was most likely bogus, seemed farfetched. True, he was used to hunting down criminals with a price on their head that generally involved gunplay, but those miscreants generally left a trail to follow, and their haunts were usually predictable. Hunting down a woman of ill repute and bringing her in merely for testimony put a wrinkle in things. Even if he were able to locate her and she was unwilling to drop whatever she was doing to go with him to Wichita, just how was he to handle things with there being no lawful warrant on her? He posed that question to Creed.

T.C. did not flinch. "In the eyes of the law, when they arrested Larry, they arrested the right person and have no interest in Lanie Brooks. My son's life is at stake, and I feel that her testimony may be enough to save him from the gallows. Warrant or no warrant, I need for her to be brought in to testify, even if she is bound and forced to come."

Judd nodded his understanding. "Well, that is a mighty generous offer you've made, T.C. I have never hunted down a woman before, but it sure sounds interesting. Let's go over to the house and explain things to my lady friend, Faye, and see what she has to say about it."

• • •

Faye had watched from the window when the stranger had ridden up. She waited until Judd and the man were walking toward the house before stepping out to greet them.

After introductions, Judd held his hand out to T.C. Creed and allowed the man to reiterate what he had said to Judd about Lanie Brooks and his offer of five thousand dollars as payment.

Faye's eyes were wide as she digested what the man had explained. "Would you mind, Mister Creed, if Judd and I had a moment alone to discuss this?" she asked. Not waiting for an answer, she looked Judd in the eye and motioned with nod of her head for him to follow, then stepped a dozen paces away.

When Judd joined her, she asked in a quiet voice, "Do you think you're ready to return to a hunt, Judd?"

Judd nodded. "I've been feeling okay, and as far as I know, I haven't had a fainting spell since the day we moved in. There's only one way to find out, and that's to get on the road and see how I handle things."

Faye was concerned and apprehensive. She'd known that this day would come, because Judd was not used to living a sedentary life. Another month or so here on the farm would have been to Judd's benefit. However, it seemed that things were happening a lot sooner than she had expected.

"Alright, then," she said. "I know that you're ready and eager to get on a trail after being stuck here looking after me. Well, I'm ready, too, and this doesn't sound like too bad a job, kind of soft, actually, for the money he is offering."

She and Judd then returned to stand in front of Creed. "And no one knows where she went or where she came from?" Faye asked.

Creed shook his head. "If I knew, I would have gone after her myself. Oh, the clerk at the hotel said that the man in question, who signed in with the name of George Wiggins, mentioned that he and the girl had traveled all day. The livery operator said that the two only had two pieces of baggage—apparently their clothing—with them, and no camping gear. By deduction, they most likely traveled from a location not so far away, such as Ellsworth or Hays in the north, but no one knows for sure. All he told me was that the tracks of the buggy she left in were headed north.

"I figured you two were my best bet." He looked at Faye. "You being a woman and all, you can go into places that your partner, Judd, and I are not allowed to go into."

Faye nodded. "Do you have a description of this Lanie Brooks? Hair color, eyes? How tall is she? How much does she weigh? How old is she?" She paused for a moment, then said, "Most likely, other girls were working the saloon that day. Did any of them talk with her prior to the shooting? Perhaps Judd and I should ride over to Great Bend and talk to the bartender and the girls, the livery operator, and such. A lot of answers are needed before Judd and I could proceed."

T.C. smiled. "You are thorough, ma'am. I'm impressed. Proves that you two take your work seriously." He added, "From what I was told by my son, Larry, Lanie Brooks is about twenty or so, about five-foot-two, 120 pounds, blonde hair, blue eyes, and a pretty face. I did talk to two girls that were entertaining others at Milt's that night. Neither girl had talked with Lanie or the deceased before the incident. They and the bartender indicated the two came in about five o'clock, perhaps timing their visit in order to work the evening crowd."

T.C. then flared a hand. "Like I explained to Judd, time is of the essence. I see no reason for you to waste a day by riding down to Great Bend. There is nothing more to add to what I've already told you. If you agree to my terms, it would most likely be wise for us to begin looking in places that the girl could have traveled to, that would be distanced no more than a day's ride by buggy, since she was not equipped to camp out."

Judd cast a wary eye to the man. "Were you planning on riding along with us, Mister Creed?"

T.C. was quick to answer. "Yes. Is that a problem, Judd?"

Judd hesitated for a moment, then shook his head. "Well, I usually work alone, never needed help. However, because of circumstances a while back, Faye and I teamed up. The way I see it, you're the one paying the bill, and because this isn't an actual bounty hunt, I reckon there's no good reason why you can't enter the hunt—provided you don't hamper our movements."

Perhaps to further explain, T.C. with a look of concern on his face said, "It's my intention to locate Miss Brooks. I'm not worried about the money I'll be advancing to you, nor will I get in the way with however you and Faye do things, Judd. I've spent a lifetime of riding and working from daylight to dark, and I'm no stranger to living out of my saddlebags."

He paused for moment, then said, "It's just that I can't stand to sit around town waiting for answers. My son's life is at stake, and I'd like to believe that I could be of help in locating Lanie Brooks and see to her testifying at the trial, perhaps saving my son's life."

Faye looked over to Judd to see if he had anything further

to add. Judd merely nodded his head in approval.

Faye then turned to face T.C. "Sounds like the perfect job for the three of us to take on, Mister Creed. We can all begin our search first thing tomorrow. But for now, I have a stew cooking, and it will be ready soon. All you and Judd need to do is wash up. Later on, you and Judd can go over any particulars. We have a spare bedroom in the house."

T.C. nodded. "The food sounds great, and it's very generous of you to offer the accommodations, but if it's okay with you, I'll bunk in the barn alongside my horse."

Judd said, "Let's go take care of your horse and wash up."

At dinner, the talk centered on allowing Creed to tell of his and his three sons' lives back on the ranch in Texas.

CHAPTER FIVE

Lanie Brooks was born and raised by her impoverished parents near the small town of Hot Springs, Arkansas. Lanie had no education to speak of, although she did finish the eighth grade. Lanie had just turned fifteen when one evening after dinner, her father called to her, "Let's take a walk, Lanie." At the time, she didn't know if she was relieved or dreaded taking the walk with him, because she pretty well knew what he was going to say.

Her home life was anything but stable. Her father was gone most of the time. He didn't have a regular job that she or her weary mother, busy raising kids, knew of. He never spoke of such, but he always seemed to have money in his pocket. She had witnessed her two older brothers walking with her father, then both having left home shortly afterward. She'd not seen Homer and Danny for over a year now. Her mother had told her that both boys were picking cotton over by McGeehee, but she she'd heard from others that Homer had fled to Texas and Danny was in jail in Indian Territory for having been caught stealing something from a mercantile.

She was actually glad to see them gone; both boys were

foul-mouthed sneaks and reprimanded almost daily for some outlandish behavior they were guilty of having done. Homer, the oldest of the two boys had raped Lanie when he was fourteen, and she but nine at the time. She had told her mother about it, thinking she would relay the abuse to her father, but neither parent ever said anything about it.

Danny caught Lanie in the barn one day and pushed her to ground in attempt to have his way with her, as well, but Lanie was able to fight off the smaller of the two boys.

When she and her father were a few steps away from the house, he began to speak. "You've had enough schooling, Lanie. It's time for you to go out and find some kinda work. You're too frail to do like your brothers and go to picking cotton, but I hear that Stella Franks is looking for a girl to wait tables at her café. Maybe you ought to go see her. It's all your ma and I can do to feed and care for your younger sisters."

Lanie didn't argue, because she knew how tight things were at home. The next morning, she headed straight to Stella's Café and asked to speak with the owner.

Stella, who had been thinking of hiring some help for her small but busy café, liked the girl's looks and said she could use Lanie to begin immediately. Stella told her, "Work starts before daylight, ends when the last customer leaves. Sometimes that's eight to nine at night. It's long hours, but a body gets used to it. I can pay you fifty cents a day, and you get your meals. If you need a place to sleep, there's an extra room with a bunk in back, and you're welcome to use it. I used to stay there before I bought a share of the Wavy Hotel, and now I have a room there."

It seemed that the job at Stella's Cafe was the perfect job

for Lanie. She worked diligently keeping things clean, and she seemed to get along well with customers. The growing amount of tips she received proved that. Lanie's looks alone were reason enough for a number of local males to be interested. Nevertheless, Lanie had not dated any of them, in particular the ones near her own age, and none of them appeared to be well off. She was fearful of ending up marrying a poor local and start having kids right away, thus ending up in the same situation as her mother had.

Perhaps for that reason, Lanie seemed more attracted to men who seemed confident but carefree and a little on the wild side.

Two years later, a handsome well-dressed man by the name of George Wiggins came into the restaurant and ordered the most expensive item on the menu. He struck up a conversation with Lanie. Wiggins had clean speech and acted genuinely interested in anything she had to say. She, in turn, liked his gentle manner. Wiggins was a man of unknown means. She figured he most likely meant spent his time playing cards at Jack's Saloon gambling for the sometimes not-so-small amount he managed to win daily. It mattered not to her how the nice man made his living—perhaps he was well off enough that he did not need to work.

George was in town for two weeks and took all his meals at Stella's Cafe. He and Lanie conversed at each of his visits and seemed to hit it off together. Lanie, now interested in the suave man, agreed to accompany him on a Sunday picnic.

A week later, Lanie waited until time to close the café for the day to announce to Stella, "George has asked me to go to Nebraska with him, said we'd get married as soon as we get settled."

Stella, though not surprised by the comely young woman's declaration, said, "Lanie, I think the world of you. Why, you're like a daughter to me. I just hope that you're not making a big mistake. Perhaps you should let George get himself settled and send for you later." Deep down, Stella knew that the girl was head over heels in love and no amount of talking was going to change her mind.

She held back from voicing her opinion of George Wiggins. Others had told her of the man's only source of income was from gambling—and that was not a recipe for a stable home life, no matter how much money he kept in his wallet. She figured that Lanie's future would soon become clouded when the man's true intentions were exposed.

As it turned out, Lanie and George never got married because they apparently never were in one place long enough to settle. For the next week, they traveled at a leisurely pace, taking all their meals in restaurants and staying in hotel rooms at night, where George satisfied his lust for the young woman, seemingly overdoing it by insisting on coupling numerous times during the night. Lanie was no prude, however, she did not get the same thrill that George did out their lovemaking.

She never turned him down and responded occasionally while he was busy on top of her, but mostly she just lay there and allowed him to do as he pleased.

It was a week later in their Kansas City hotel room that George said to Lanie, "Let's go down to the KC Saloon and have a drink."

George ordered drinks for the two of them and told the bartender to keep them coming. Lanie had never drunk any spirits before but sipped at the wine that George had ordered for her. It wasn't bad, she admitted, and before long was taking larger sips from her second glass.

Then, George said, "Time for me to get busy. You just wait here, Lanie, I'll be over at that card game." He pointed to a table where five men sat playing cards.

Another drink arrived to her before she had finished the second one and she was feeling the effects of the alcohol. A half-hour later, she was tipsy and smiling when George took a seat next to her. "A fella is going to come over and keep you company while I'm busy, Lanie. When you're ready, he'll escort you up to our room." Lanie stared in wonderment as George stood. "Don't worry, everything's going to work out, you'll see." He then added, "We all got to do our part."

The drinks fogged Lanie's brain. Still, she wondered at what George meant by his parting comment.

Two minutes after George returned to the gambling table, a man seated next to him stood, looked in her direction, then walked over to Lanie's table. He was an older man, perhaps forty, dressed in a vested blue suit and shiny boots. He had neatly combed hair and a broad smile on his face.

The man pulled out a chair then sat down beside Lanie. "Hi, I'm Corbett Minns." Lanie shook his extended hand. The man then said, "You're a pretty lady. George is one lucky man."

Minns held a hand up to the barkeeper to order more drinks. Before Lanie could voice a protest, the drinks arrived.

A few minutes later, Lanie felt the man's hand on her knee. She looked over to George's table, knowing that he was plainly able to see her and the man fondling her leg under the table. George merely raised his glass in a salute, then turned his attention to the card game.

Drunk as she was, she understood; George wanted her to become a whore in order to pay for her living expenses. All her illusions of wedded bliss vanished. She thought about walking out and leaving the rat, but where would she go? What would she do? She could not go back to Stella's, nor were there any thoughts of returning to her childhood home. No, in each instance, it had been time for her to make a move and she had made the decision to leave. Now, she had to face the consequences.

Money-wise, she was flat broke. She had given all her money to George a few days ago because she knew it was expensive to live on the road and she wanted to pay her part, but apparently, that was not enough. She had totally trusted in her new beau, but now, he had betrayed her. She wondered if she could ever trust any man. Were they all rotten to the core, only interested in satisfying their immediate wants or lusts? All her feelings for George went out the window.

She contemplated her situation for a moment, then realized that this is what George wanted and expected of her all along. He had recruited her—not out of love—but figured to use her for his own gain. He wanted her to sleep with other men for money. Not something she had ever considered.

Well, if that was the way things were, so be it, she had always been able to handle the changes that life brought to her. Right now, she did not have a choice—she had to do as George willed. She also knew that there were consequences for every action, and someday George would pay dearly for what he had set her up to do.

Minns said, "Whenever you're ready, pretty lady, I am."

Lanie stood, then walked to the stairs with Minns right behind her.

She was without any feelings when she allowed Minns to do as he wished with her. Afterward, Minns dressed, then said, "I already paid George, but this is a little extra for you." He then laid a five-dollar bill on a table then left the room. Lanie secreted the money, figuring she needed to build a stash for future use.

She was sleeping soundly and did not awaken when George returned to the room. The next morning, neither spoke as they dressed, then went to the restaurant for breakfast.

She broke the silence by asking, "Are we still going to Nebraska, George?"

The man nodded. "We'll be here for a week," George said nonchalantly, as if it was just business as usual. "I have two paying customers lined up for you tonight already."

As George had said, they stayed in Kansas City for the week and Lanie entertained more clients each night. They then left town, heading in a northern direction.

It seemed that George was quite happy the way Lanie had taken to his plan without complaint. She, on the other hand, had plans of her own; she would keep quiet about what occupied her thoughts. It might take some time before she could take any definitive action.

The next stop was St. Joseph, Missouri. It was business as usual for a week, then they were off heading north again. In their travel, they followed a route that George was familiar with but never disclosed to her their next destination. They would spend one, sometimes two nights in one small town, then another, moving on only when George had figured that between his gambling and her whoring, they had taken all they were going to get.

They did make it to Nebraska, but apparently, there was no definite location that George had hinted of back when they first met. They would spend a night in a low-class hotel, while George scouted out potential clients, then the next day move on to another small town. Their travels took them westward, then southwest to Denver, where they spent two weeks before moving on to Colorado Springs. For the next six months, it was a dizzying journey for Lanie, one town after the other, in a nowhere route that circled through Colorado, Nebraska, Missouri, and Kansas.

Each stop amounted to a repeat of the same thing they had just left; they would check into a hotel, have a meal, then head to a nearby saloon where George would set things up for the night. He would do his gambling and line up clients for Lanie for the evening.

Her loathing for George increased with each passing day. It finally reached a peak one day in Wichita when one morning George said to her at breakfast, "I had a streak of bad luck last night, need to borrow the money you have stashed." She was astounded. For one thing, she didn't think he knew of the stash of tips she had kept hidden from him; and for the second, she did not believe he wanted to *borrow* the money. No, he had most likely wanted her to contribute it to his pocket, and she would never see the money again.

That did it! She had had enough of his lying, sneaking ways, and turning her into a whore. She desperately wanted to get away from him or kill him, and she would feel no remorse for doing so.

She did not know how to do it without suffering an arrest

afterward...maybe get a hold of a gun, shoot him out on the trail away from town, and then swear to law officers that some miscreant had robbed them and killed him. She had never handled a gun before—no need to. Oh, she had watched as her two brothers had shot rabbits and squirrels, but she herself had never shot a gun.

That didn't matter to her; she had watched her brothers firing their rifles plenty of times and figured she could pull a trigger if she could get ahold of a gun. She did not care how she did, but some way, she had to escape from George.

She made up her mind that she would kill him. She would bide her time until the right chance came along, then she would take it.

That very opportunity happened shortly afterward in Great Bend when the young cowboy she was sitting with drew his six-gun on George. She reacted to the situation as if instructed to push that cowboy's arm hard enough to cause him to fire his weapon. She would have gladly pulled the trigger herself, if the gun were in her hand.

CHAPTER SIX

Lanie Brooks was frightened, but relieved, when she fled from Great Bend. It was dark out, and she was alone and wanted to remain so. She knew she had to be careful because there were all kinds of miscreant travelers who would not hesitate to take advantage—possibly use, then kill, a lone woman out on the trail. For that reason, she traveled all night, only stopping to water and rest the horse briefly, and then travel again.

By daylight, she knew she was near Ellsworth. She planned to get the horse cared for, then check into the Ellsworth Inn, the place she and George had stayed each time they came to town. Once her head hit the pillow that evening, she was immediately asleep and slept throughout the day.

She awakened at about the time it had gotten dark. She lay on the bed and attempted to get her thoughts together. She needed a plan. She wanted to put some distance from where George had been shot, and to begin a new life without the cad.

There was about two hundred dollars in George's wallet,

which was hers to begin with—the remnants of her tip money he had taken. That would get her by for a while. She didn't feel like hunting for another food server job. That would be just marking time again. She didn't mind whoring, now that she had been at it for a time. The men meant nothing to her, they only had their own pleasure in mind, and she did what she had to do to hurry things to conclusion. If she continued on whoring for a time anyway, she could at least keep all the profits.

However, she did not want to travel from town to town as George had insisted on doing.

There were too many dangers for a woman alone. She was well aware of many potential problems, and purposely saw to staying out of harm's way.

George never spent the night camping out, but rather always moved along to find a roadhouse to bunk in, possibly do a little business before bedtime. In addition, they always stayed in a halfway decent place. George proved that he was either concerned for her welfare or he was just fussy.

She remembered one time when they had stopped at a shabby-looking roadhouse about an hour out from Wichita. The odor of stale beer, men's sweat, tobacco juice, and cigar smoke permeated the air as they stepped inside. Before the bar stood five rough-looking characters, either local drovers or those on the prowl, all wearing big six-guns holstered on one hip. All eyes followed them until she and George seated themselves at one of four tables. George stepped to order them both drinks. When George sat down, he said, "We won't be long; just have the drink, then travel on. Never been here before and I just wanted to see what the place looked like inside."

In a short time, two rough-looking men, wearing dirty, rumpled clothes, and a young, plain looking girl of seventeen or so took the table next to them. She was a pudgy girl, with light-colored hair to her shoulders. She wore a threadbare but clean light blue dress that hit her legs at mid-calf. The girl swept her wide-open, big blue eyes around the room as she took a seat. She fidgeted in her chair, obviously not used to the surroundings, and perhaps frightened.

One man sat beside the girl and the other sat across the table from her. Both men wore rumpled, dirty shirts and faded jeans, scarred boots, and jingling spurs. The men wore frayed slouch hats and looked as if they had not shaved in a week or so.

The one sitting next to the girl said, "I'll get the drinks, Moses. What should I get for her?"

The man across from the girl said, "Hell, Jiggs, get her a shot of Old Clegg. She might as well break in right off."

When Jiggs returned with the drinks, he set a full shot glass in front of the girl. He also placed a glass of beer and a full shot glass in front of Moses, then took his seat beside the girl, raised a hand, and began rubbing her shoulder. He then pointed across the table. "Moses will show you the best way to get the most benefit from your drink, Sally."

Moses grinned and nodded, then said, "You've had a rough time of it, Sally, losing your pa and all. I promised your aunt Mag that we would take you to town and see to getting your mind off things for a time, show you a good time."

He then picked up his shot glass. "Just throw it all back in one gulp. Trust me on this," he implored. "That little drink will make you feel better—good, in fact—and help to take your mind off things for a while."

He then brought his shot glass to within a few inches of his lips, tilted his head, then dashed the contents into his mouth and swallowed. He sat back in his chair and declared, "See, nothing to it. Now, you'll know why your daddy always was partial to the stuff."

"Go ahead and try it," Jiggs encouraged.

Sally looked at the shot glass then reached and picked it up and held it in front of her face.

"Lower it down in front of your lips," Moses instructed. When she had it in the right position, he said, "Okay, now, dash the whole thing into your mouth just like you seen me do."

Sally opened her mouth wide, then did as instructed, and sent the liquid into her mouth.

It seemed as if instantly all hell had broken loose. Within a scant few seconds of swallowing the whiskey, Sally jumped to her feet and sent a stream of puke across the table into Moses's face. An automatic reaction allowed no time for her to turn away before losing the contents of her stomach. Moses attempted to turn sideways too late, and he began vomiting as well.

George stood and said to Lanie, "Time for us to leave."

Moses was cussing and howling profanities as George and Lanie stepped outside. They mounted the carriage and set off. Lanie often wondered what became of Sally. She hoped the poor girl, obviously naïve to the ways of the scoundrels who were attempting to lead her astray, would go back to her aunt Mag's home much wizened.

Lanie made up her mind that she would not travel around to patronize any low-class joints, which drew in those such as Moses and Jiggs, filthy of mind and body.

Settling into one decent place, with clean surroundings as well as clean customers, was more appealing; a place she could settle into and call home. She wracked her brain until she remembered that she and George had spent a few nights in Kansas City, and stayed in a decent hotel.

George had gambled and she had seen to a few men's needs at The Red Carpet Gaming House. She recalled the bartender, a kindly man, named Harlow who had delivered a drink to her table where she sat alone. He had said, "You're too pretty to be traveling around with George all the time, missy. The girls that work here do quite well without the hassle of traveling all over. Too bad George doesn't take root for a while."

She wondered if that was an invitation, and if the man were still there and how he would be to work with. Well, with nothing else on the horizon, she would just have to pay the man a visit and see. Maybe she and he could work out a deal. With George out of the way, it would be up for negotiation as to the amount of profits she would be able to keep for her services, taking into consideration expenses such as room and board that the man would surely charge. However, there were things to take care of first. She would go and find a meal, then retire back to the room and rest up until morning, then do what was necessary in order to put her plan into action.

• • •

She was awake the next morning before daylight, well rested and ready to go. While at breakfast at the hotel restaurant, the waitress answered her inquiry of where the stage office was located. Lanie bought a ticket to Abilene. She and George had been there several times and always did well there. She would lounge overnight until time to board the stage to Topeka the following day, and later on, eventually, make her way to Kansas City—and hopefully, to a more palatable new beginning. The route she chose was the same that she and George had traveled previously. It was familiar territory, and she could travel in somewhat more comfortable conditions without facing the elements in an open buggy.

Next, she went to the A-1 Livery, where she had stabled the mare, and made a deal for the owner to buy the horse and buggy. She knew the man took advantage by offering her a mere forty dollars for both. She was not in a position to argue, and agreed. She had no further use for either, and did not need the hassle of caring for the horse.

CHAPTER SEVEN

The next morning, Lanie was waiting at the stage depot when the 10:00 o'clock stage arrived. The driver announced that they would be leaving for Salina in a half-hour. He then busied himself bringing buckets of water to set before each of the four horses, then checked the animals' shoes and hooves.

Lanie was quite bored and anxious to leave. She had spent her time here mostly in her room, venturing out only for food. She felt no desire to wander into the local saloons at night and offer her services; she'd made up her mind that since George was no longer in the picture, she would not go back to entertaining gentlemen in one saloon after another unless she had to—and right now, she did not have to.

Her objective was to get to Kansas City and see if Harlow was receptive to making a deal with her. It was her intention to simplify things, eliminate travel, settle into one neat and clean place, and be able to call it home. There were too many grungy men in some of the saloons she and George had visited on the road, but the clientele at the Red Carpet Gaming House in Kansas City seemed refined and clean. She had big hopes that she would not be disappointed once she got there and talked with Harlow.

Lanie watched as a tall man mounted the stage with a shotgun in hand. The shotgun rider took a seat as the stage driver opened the stage door and called out, "We're ready to go, folks!"

Lanie, followed by an another much older, frail-looking woman, stepped into the coach and took seats next to each other.

"I'm Mildred Carnes," the woman said.

"Lanie Brooks," Lanie said, as two men dressed in suit jackets and bowler hats, obviously drummers of some sort, climbed in, as well. Both men had grins on their faces when they tipped their hats and introduced themselves to Lanie, while ignoring the older Mildred Carnes.

Lanie nodded, then merely said, "I'm Lanie." She then turned to look out the coach window as the driver climbed the stage.

The man took his seat, then called out to the team, "Giddy up!" and the stage lurched forward.

Afterward, both the drummers attempted in vain to strike up a conversation with Lanie. Lanie would answer each of their questions with short, curt answers, then resume looking out her window. It did not take long before the only sounds heard were the commands of the driver to his team and the rumbling of the coach as it traveled along.

Two hours later, the stage slowed to cross Grimes Creek and to take a sharp right turn onto the road heading east. As soon as the stage had made the turn, the driver yelled out, "Whoa!" and brought the coach to a stop.

In the roadway before the stage were three masked men

mounted on horses. Greg Henderson, Lars O'Hansen and Manny Wilkes were former drovers for the Ivers Brand Ranch from northwest Texas. They had been part of the crew that delivered a herd of cattle to Ellsworth.

Greg Henderson was a lifelong criminal, thug, thief, and killer. He had stolen candy at age five. By the time, he was sixteen, he was rolling drunks in darkened alleys for the contents of their pockets. He knocked one such drunken man in the head a little too hard and the man died on the spot, but Greg didn't care. He'd gotten the man's money—eighteen dollars—his pocket watch, and a fine-looking .36 caliber cap and ball Colt Navy revolver.

The Colt was a beauty, and fully loaded with balls and percussion caps in place—the only problem being reloads. If he shot all six shots then without a supply of lead, powder, and caps at his disposal, he would be defenseless. Greg decided he would not shoot the weapon unless his life was threatened or if he had to during, say, a stickup he was pulling.

He later exchanged the six-gun for a .44 Colt pistol that took metallic cartridges. Greg would only work for wages as a last resort if his money ran out and there was nothing available to steal. Three months ago, he found himself in that predicament and that was when he had signed on to make the cattle drive, simply because he needed to eat.

Lars O'Hansen was also a thief, though never caught and charged with a crime because he usually had a job of some sort and used that fact to cover his actions. Lars did not think ahead, but would react to whatever the current circumstance was. He was not lazy and always did as directed by others.

When his former employer died, Lars was at a loss as to what to do next until a friend suggested he ride out to the IB Ranch. Lars signed on this past spring and informed them that he would be part of the crew herding the cattle to Ellsworth.

Manny Wilkes's fingers were not very sticky—or rather, he did not bother with petty thievery. He was not above doing a little larceny, provided he felt safe in covering his tracks. He was mild-mannered and not much of a gun hand, only wearing a six-gun for show. He had never shot anyone, or even faced a belligerent who wanted to do battle. He did his job handling the cattle, but he had no business siding up with the miscreant Greg Henderson.

• • •

The cattle buyer met with rancher Kurt Ivers and paid cash for the herd of over five hundred head. Afterward, Ivers summoned the crew to a room just off the hotel's lobby where he sat at a table and waited for each man to step forward to collect his pay in cash.

Ivers was a tough man to work for and tight with his money, trusting no one. Each of the drovers received his eighty-seven dollars pay and nothing more for eighty-seven days of pushing the herd. Ivers did not even shake any of the men's hands or offer to buy them a drink, let alone provide any bonus money for the job. All that made for hard feelings toward Ivers.

Manny, Lars, and Greg took their pay, then walked across the street to The Aces Saloon. After ordering drinks, Manny swore that he would never work for the man again. Lars bobbed his head in agreement, but that was not good enough for Greg, who then said, "I think we ought to teach that old bastard a lesson."

"What do you have in mind, Greg?" Manny asked.

"Well, hell, we brought over five hundred head of cattle to town. I don't know how much Ivers sold them for, but a fellow in the know said the going price was nineteen to twenty-two dollars a head. That means he has at least ten thousand dollars in his pocket. I figure he could have at least paid each of us a hundred dollars for the daylight-to-dark work we did getting that herd here, and there wouldn't be any of us with hard feelings."

He paused for a moment, then continued. "I've known Kurt Ivers for some time—long before you and Lars came along. He trusts no one when it comes to money, including the banks. I would be willing to bet that he will not put the money he got for the herd in the bank. He'll keep his hands on it until he can figure out how to get it out of town to where he figures it'll be safe without anyone knowing where it went."

Manny rolled a shoulder. "So he's distrusting...so what?"

Greg glared at him. "We ought to find a way to take it away from him."

"How are you gonna to do that when there's law in this town?" Manny asked.

Greg flared a hand outward. "It could end up real simple. All we gotta do is watch what Ivers does while he's in town. That way, we can see what he'll be doing to disguise the money. Once we know what to look for, it's just a matter of keeping track of the money. We wait until someone leaves town with the money, then we follow and take it."

"What makes you so sure Ivers will do that?" Manny asked.

Greg retorted, "Because, he's done it before. Happened after the first drive I made for him, three years ago. That time, we delivered a herd to Wichita. Ivers paid everyone off. Later on, I learned from a fellow drover who overheard Ivers talking to a kid of about fourteen with a plan for his money."

He repeated what Ivers had said to the kid. *"All's you got to do is take these saddlebags and ride south down to Arkansas City. Do not tell anyone where you are going or why. It will take you two days of riding about thirty miles a day. There will be no camping out. First thing in the morning, you can take off and ride to Wellington, where you will spend the night at the Third Street Hotel. I have already arranged for you to stay the night. The next morning, you can ride on down to Arkansas City. I'll meet you at the City Hotel and take the bags back."*

Greg continued, "Leopards don't change their spots and I don't figure Ivers will change his ways, either."

Greg, Manny and Lars, at Greg's insistence, spent the day watching every move that Kurt Ivers made with disappointing results. Ivers did not appear to do anything out of the ordinary, but Greg was wary. He just knew the man would do something about secreting his money out of town, and that happened about mid-morning when the three former drovers watched as Ivers crossed the street to the stage office.

Greg immediately told Manny and Lars, "Time to go fetch our horses and get ready to ride." They had left their horses behind the hotel, with saddle cinches loosened, close by if needed in a hurry.

A few minutes later, the stage pulled up in front of the depot. Greg watched while the driver opened up the luggage compartment in the back of the coach and began placing baggage from the two women and two men passengers inside. That was when Kurt Ivers came out of the stage office and handed a small, ordinary-looking leather satchel to the driver, who placed it inside with the other baggage, then pulled the cover down and lashed it closed. Ivers talked briefly with the driver, then moved away.

So that's it, Greg surmised, *he's sending the money out of town on the stage without any fanfare. No special guard, unless one of those male passengers is traveling incognito.*

"Let's go," Greg said to Manny and Lars as they arrived with Greg's horse in tow.

"Where are we going?" Manny asked.

"We need to find a good place, a ways from town, where we can stop that stage. I figure that Ivers intended to hide the money and sneak it out of town without anyone being the wiser. I just watched him put a satchel in with the stage's baggage. We need to see what's inside that satchel."

The three rode their horses hard for a distance until they came to Grimes Creek. They stopped long enough to water themselves and their horses. A few minutes later when they walked the horses across the creek and the road took a sharp turn to the right, Greg held up a hand. "This is as good a place as any. We must be about ten miles from town. We can wait right here for them. They ought to be along soon and will have to go slow to make the turn. We won't even have to chase them down. Once they're stopped, Manny, you fire off a shot to get their attention while Lars and I cover the passengers."

When they heard the rattling stage, the three would-be robbers tied bandanas over their noses and mouths. They then mounted up. Greg, Lars, and Manny positioned their horses in the middle of the road and waited.

When the driver had brought the coach to a stop before the three masked men, neither the driver nor shotgun rider said anything.

Each of the three men had a lever-action Winchester, with the muzzles pointed up and the stocks resting on a leg. Greg and Lars guided their horses to either side of the coach. Both riders pointed their Winchesters toward the coach. The remaining man in front, Manny Wilkes, pulled the trigger of his rifle, the shot going into the air meant as a warning.

Manny then said loudly to the shotgun rider, "Best leave that scattergun where it sits, mister."

The shotgun rider lifted his hands.

The driver called out, "What do you men want? We ain't even carrying a strongbox."

Wilkes jacked a fresh round into his smoking carbine while Greg answered. "No, but you got a satchel in the boot put there by Kurt Ivers back in Ellsworth. I seen him hand it to you, and you tossed it in with the other baggage. We intend to have it. Now, step down and open up the back."

The driver then said, "You men are going through a lot of trouble just for a bag. Why don't you just wait and pick it up when we get to Salina?"

Greg replied immediately, "Because we want it right now!"

The driver then tied the reins to his brake handle and began climbing down. The shotgun rider must have figured that he could get them out of this fix and made a sudden move for his scattergun. That turned out to be a costly mistake. The man began swinging the shotgun toward Manny Wilkes out front when the still mounted man on the right side of the coach, Greg Henderson, spied the movement and immediately swung the muzzle of his Winchester to center on the guard's chest and pulled the trigger.

The roar of the gun was deafening. The bullet hit the man in the center of his chest and exploded his heart as it traveled through. The unfortunate shotgun rider, who had stood, dropped the scattergun then fell forward over the side of the coach, his head striking the front wheel as his lifeless body hit the ground.

The stage driver shook his fist. "Murdering bastards!"

Greg dismounted and stood to the side to keep watch over the fallen guard and to watch the reactions of those inside the coach.

The rider still in front of the coach, Manny Wilcox, had quieted after Greg had shot the guard. He grimaced, then scolded, "Damn it, Greg, I thought that we all agreed on doing this without any bloodshed. Now, look at what you've done. The driver and those inside seen it all and will tell the law for sure."

"Damn right we will," the driver muttered.

Greg ratcheted another round into his Winchester, then turned the muzzle to the driver and pulled the trigger. The bullet struck the man in the right side of his face, just below his eye, killing him instantly. Greg cast his eyes to his mounted partner. "Dead men cain't tell no tales."

He then said, "Why don't you and Lars go and get the satchel and check for any other valuables back there while I take care of the passengers."

He then turned to the coach. "You in there—I want you all to step out of the stage with your hands in the air...and they better be empty."

The two drummers came out first, white-faced and with their hands in the air, as he'd commanded. One of them pleaded, "We ain't got much, but you can sure have what's in our pockets. We won't say nothing to nobody, mister, if you'll just leave us be!"

Greg waited until the two women had stepped out. He looked both women over, paying slight attention to Mildred Carnes, but seeming to study Lanie at length.

Manny called out, "I got it! Want me to open it up and look?"

"Yes," Greg answered. "Lars, I want you to come over here and frisk these men's pockets for weapons and anything worth us taking."

When Lars had two watches and a derringer in hand, along with twenty-three dollars and some pocket change, he said, "That's all they got. Want me to check those women, too?"

Greg wagged his head. "I'll take care of that!" He then walked over to Mildred Carnes and said, "You got any valuables?"

The woman held her purse out. "Eight dollars, and my watch."

Greg said, "Keep it." He then stepped to stand before Lanie Brooks.

• • •

Lanie glared at him, then held her purse out. "Twelve dollars and change." She had previously secreted two hundred dollars, the bulk of her funds, in the top of her stocking on her right side, but she held the hope that this rough-looking man would not strip her and find it.

Greg grinned. "Traveling kinda light, are we?" He smirked but made no move to take the purse. He then stepped to put his left arm around her waist and pulled her to press against him. He began to run his right hand all over her back and bottom, then gave a squeeze to each of her breasts.

After what seemed to Lanie an endless time, Greg finally stepped back. Then, without saying a word, he lifted his six-gun and began pulling the trigger. She watched in shocked horror as the lifeless bodies of her fellow passengers dropped to the ground. He had shot each of the drummers and Mildred Carnes so quickly that no one was able to make a move to escape. All three crumpled to the ground, twitching as life left them.

Lanie waited for a bullet to take her life, as well. Instead, Greg said to her, "You'll be coming along with me."

Lars remained silent, as he often did, but Manny was beside himself. "What you done is bad, Greg!" he said loudly. "There was no need to kill all those folks. I'm just sick over it. We got the money in the satchel, and it looks like a lot to me."

Greg was quick to answer, "Hell, that shotgunner is to blame! He was gonna shoot either you or me with that scattergun. I did you a favor by stopping him."

"What about the driver and those passengers? They didn't do anything," Manny whined.

"There ain't no witnesses to point a finger at us," Greg retorted. "And like you say, we got the loot—and nobody knows that but us. Now, we can ride off and go where we want without having anyone dogging our tracks."

Manny pointed at Lanie. "What about her?"

Greg flared a hand. "She's with me. You won't say a word, will you, sweet thing?"

Lanie could only shake her head, secretly in disgust rather than agreement.

CHAPTER EIGHT

Judd had already mounted as he waited for Faye and T.C. Creed to mount their horses. He said, "I figure we should head north like you said Miss Brooks most likely did, T.C.—maybe ride up to Hays first, see if she showed up there. If not, then we can work our way eastward toward Ellsworth. Perhaps Miss Brooks is working her way along and may have stayed over at one of the small towns strung out between Hays and Ellsworth."

It turned out to be a fruitless all-day ride. The trio canvassed every roadhouse and saloon along the way without anyone having seen Lanie Brooks, or a lone woman in a buggy, passing through. It was the same in Hays, though Neil at Rosie's House, a house of ill repute, knew who Lanie Brooks was. When asked, he said, "As far as I know, she and George haven't been here for a month or so. In addition, you say George caught a bullet and died. Some unhappy customer, I suppose."

"Something like that," T.C. retorted, then added, "and we're just trying to locate her because she is a witness to the shooting."

It had been a long day, so Judd said, "Well, looks like she must have turned off and driven over to Ellsworth instead. We might as well spend the night. In the morning, we can get an early start and check what places we come to along the way. I figure it'll still take us two days to reach Ellsworth." He gave a glance to T.C., then said encouragingly, "This man or uh—*woman* hunting sometimes takes time, but sooner or later we're bound to pick up her trail."

• • •

They arrived in Ellsworth late in the day, two days later. All their riding and stops had ended the same as when they had ridden to Hays. Things brightened up when they questioned a bald-headed clerk at the Ellsworth Inn when they checked in and explained why they were looking for Lanie Brooks.

The man nodded. "Yeah, I recall that Miss Brooks was here for a couple nights then left some three or four days ago. She never said where she was going, and I didn't ask. Too bad about old George...he always paid his bill with no complaints."

T.C. Creed nodded his understanding. "Did you happen to notice if she drove away in a buggy?"

The man shook his head. "She walked out with a small bag in hand is all I know, but if she had a horse and buggy, you might try the A-1 Livery, just down the street. Ole Harley might know; he always sends anyone coming to town and looking for a room to see us. Fact is, you can walk your animals over to his place and leave them in his corral overnight; there's a water trough and plenty of hay he leaves out for any nighttime arrivals. He's most likely gone home by now, but he'll take care of your stock come daylight."

"Thanks," T.C. offered. He then turned to face Judd and Faye. "Why don't you two get yourselves situated in your room. I'll take the horses over to the livery, then meet you in the hotel's restaurant in a short time."

Judd replied, "What the hell, T.C., it's been a long day for you, too. I think we ought to take our horses over to the livery and get them situated, then we can all go get a bite to eat. We'll find out where she went come morning. At least she hasn't started using a different name, yet."

• • •

After breakfast the next morning, the three searchers walked to the livery and identified themselves to Ole Harley. "The man over at the Ellsworth Inn sent us here last night so we went ahead and turned our horses into your corral. Now we're here to settle up."

The man grinned. "Ain't no problem, folks. With hay, water, and oats and the keep for three hosses, I figure five dollars ought to cover it." Seemed a little high to Judd, but he did not comment.

While T.C. was paying the bill, Judd said, "I see you got a buggy in your yard. So happens we're looking for the owner of buggy like that. A young woman, in fact. We know that she was in town a few days ago."

Harley nodded. "I bought that buggy and the horse that pulled it from a nice, pretty, young lady a short time ago. She didn't give me her name or say why she was selling it. She just seemed relieved at not having to care for them any longer. Maybe that's the woman you are looking for but I haven't seen her since. She must have left town, might have taken the stage."

Judd shook his head. "As far as I know, she owned the buggy and was free to sell it." He felt no need to explain why they were looking for Lanie Brooks.

Their next stop was the stage depot. T.C. and Judd waited outside when Faye volunteered to enter the tiny office. A slight woman with gray hair sat behind the ticket counter.

Faye greeted the woman clerk, then inquired if a woman by the description of Lanie Brooks had left town on a recent stage. When she got a frown from the woman, obviously not accustomed to providing information about customers, Faye explained. "I can assure you that our reasons for locating her are for good intentions only, and we mean her no harm. We're looking for her for the simple reason that the lady in question, name of Lanie Brooks, was witness to a shooting down in Great Bend a short time ago. She disappeared right after the shooting. The life of the young man arrested for the shooting depends on the testimony she could give at the trial. The defendant's father is right outside and is desperate to locate the lady in time for the trial." She paused for a moment, then continued. "All we'd like to know is if she left on one of your stages and when. It would be most helpful if we knew the destination."

The clerk nodded her head in understanding. "Miss Brooks purchased a ticket to Abilene. I was witness to her boarding that stage the next day. That stage left here two days ago."

Faye was going to thank the woman and leave, but the

clerk stood and stepped to the window.

"Have you been by the sheriff's office?"

Faye shook her head.

The woman frowned again. "You should go and talk with the sheriff's office. I'm sorry to report that the stage suffered some problems some ten miles northeast of here.

"Apparently, it was carrying a large amount of money. The owner used the stage to transfer the funds to himself in Salina without telling us that the money was in our luggage compartment. Otherwise, we could have taken precautionary measures. All I have learned so far is that the driver and shotgun rider, along with two male passengers and one female passenger, all died from bullet wounds. A second female passenger is missing and presumed taken hostage."

When Faye stepped outside, Judd held up a hand. "We heard. So, let's go over to the sheriff's office and get the particulars."

Creed's brow furrowed as he shook his head. "This chase is getting more complicated."

Sheriff Winfred Hayes was sitting behind his desk when the trio walked in. "Howdy, folks. What can I help you with?"

Judd made brief introductions, then told of their mission. He then reiterated what the depot clerk had told them. "We're curious if Miss Brooks was taken hostage or among the deceased?"

Hayes nodded his understanding. "I can tell you all that I know. The female who died at the site was Missus Mildred Carnes, so we can assume that it was Miss Brooks taken hostage by the killers. So far, we don't know where we should begin our search for her.

"A traveler came upon the stage a couple of hours after the massacre happened and reported it to us. I immediately formed a posse, and we went looking. Two men of the posse volunteered to collect the bodies and brought the stage back here.

"The others and I found three sets of tracks leading away right on down the road the stage had been heading. We lost the tracks a few miles further on the road toward Salina. There's a lot of traffic on that road making it impossible to pick out any one set of tracks.

"We rode on into Salina and checked with the marshal there, as well as all the saloons, in hopes we would find at least one of the culprits foolishly celebrating. However, we had no such luck, so we had no choice but to come back home.

"We don't know how many robbers—killers—there were; I assume three. We found just the three sets of tracks, and that was all. If we only knew who we were looking for, it would surely help. We do have a description of the missing Miss Brooks. I've two deputies still out...they'll ride as far as Abilene, do some checking for anyone blowing a bunch of money, and keeping an eye out for Miss Brooks before they come home."

The sheriff grimaced, then said in disgust, "With nothing to go on, about all we can do is to wait and hope that someone may know something about the case and will come forward and provide us some sort of lead to follow."

Judd spoke up. "The depot clerk said someone was sending a large amount of cash in the luggage without the stage people knowing about it."

Sheriff Hayes grimaced. "That skinflint, Kurt Ivers, did that. He come storming in here as soon as the word got out about the stage robbery and began demanding to know what we were doing about it. I could not resist, and told him off. It was because of his distrust of the banks and figuring to squirrel his money out of town without anyone knowing about it that caused the robbery and massacre to begin with.

"What the hell, he didn't even let our office know what he was doing! So, when it comes to his money, I really couldn't care less. However, we still need to find those killers, and if and when we do and we recover any of the money, we will turn it over to him. I'm still trying to figure out if I can charge him with something and arrest him."

Judd digested all the sheriff had said, then said, "So, this fellow Ivers figured that no one in town knew of his putting the money inside the luggage on the stage. Very clever—if, in fact, no one else knew what he had done. But, I think it is rather obvious that someone witnessed Ivers's delivery of the parcel to the stage and that 'someone' is most likely the robbers."

The sheriff bobbed his head. "I believe that you're correct, Judd. Ivers swears that no one but himself knew, and that he was watchful but saw no one even looking in his direction when he put the satchel on the stage. We canvassed the entire town, questioning everyone in the saloons, bartenders, whores, customers, hotel clerks, business owners, and even the town drunks—and we came up empty."

Judd nodded. "Do you know where we would find Ivers? I'd like to speak with him."

Sheriff Hayes threw out a hand. "He's most likely still at the Main Street Hotel pouting. It's just down the street." He pointed to the right. "He was belligerent when I talked with him, but maybe he's settled some by now."

When the three of them stepped outside, Judd said, "Someone had to have observed Ivers putting the money on the stage; he just didn't see them. Could be one of his own men was doing the watching. Let's go find Ivers and talk to him."

They found Kurt Ivers seated at a table in the saloon of the Main Street Hotel with a drink glass before him. He scowled when the three approached.

Judd introduced himself. "Mr. Ivers, I'm Judd Jacoby." He flared a hand. "My associates, Faye McJunkin and T.C. Creed. We'd like to speak with you about the stage robbery. Specifically, we're attempting to locate the woman taken hostage from the stage hold up. We're bounty hunters."

Ivers glared at Judd, then said, "Bounty hunters! She must be worth some dough!"

Judd nodded, then said, "Actually, she was witness to a shooting, and we need to locate her."

Ivers frowned. "I don't know how I can help you. I know nothing of that woman. If you're going looking for those that took my money, I'll talk with you, but I'm not offering any bounty on my own money. I expect the law to recover it."

Judd held a chair out for Faye, then he took a seat as T.C. took a chair, as well. Judd said, "As I understand it, according to the sheriff, you secreted a satchel containing a large amount of money onto the stage in the baggage compartment?"

Ivers bobbed his head. "I didn't want anyone to know about the money. There are too many miscreants about."

"Well, it's rather obvious that someone knew. What about your own men?" Judd responded.

Ivers glared at him. "The cook and the regulars that I kept on headed back to the ranch the morning after I paid them their wages. Three others hired just for the trip, I let go. I had no reason to keep them on. The last I seen of them they were heading to the saloon down the street. You think they might have had something to do with stealing my money?"

Judd nodded. "It's possible."

Ivers frowned, then proclaimed, "Shit! It's hard for me to believe that my own men would turn on me! The sheriff asked me the same question. Moreover, as I told him, they signed up just for the drive. I've used two of them before. No reason to suspect them of any chicanery; they did their jobs of herding the cattle and knew how much pay they would get at the end of the drive.

"Men like that never seem to have any ambition to strike out on their own, content to do as directed by others. They work all day, spend their nights thinking about saloon girls and a few drinks. When payday comes along, they rush to the nearest saloon and piss their money away on booze, girls, and gambling. Hell, some won't even take the time to buy new clothes or boots, wear the same ones until they are falling apart. They will most likely be around when I am ready for the next drive. At the sheriff's insistence, I gave him their names. But like I told him, I believe those three most likely celebrated for one or two nights and then left town."

"What are their names? Judd asked.

Ivers rattled the names off. "If I had reason to suspect any of them, I'd say that Greg Henderson was the cockiest. He always had a strange look in his eyes whenever I passed out orders. Lars O'Hansen is a rough looking guy. He did an all right job, but he was too quiet...kinda spooky, in fact. Of the three, Manny Wilkes seemed out of place. Not much of a cattle herder, but he did a good enough job for me. He was mild-mannered and easily led by others, I figured."

"Do you know where those men came from?" Judd asked.

Ivers shook his head. "They each just showed up to the ranch individually at different times when word got out that I was making a drive. I've used Henderson and O'Hansen before. It was the first time for Wilkes."

"Can you describe them for us?" Judd asked.

Ivers did so, giving specific details of their sizes, heights, weights, and eye and hair color, but did not recall any distinguishing scars or handicaps that would set them apart.

He then grimaced. "Come to think on it, it *could* be those three did the robbery, but I don't see how any one of them knew about my putting the money on the stage. The sheriff said there were three sets of tracks leaving the stage. If it were those men, I would say that Greg Henderson was the leader. He must have figured to get his hands on the money and conned the other two into going along with his plan. He and others know that I am extra careful with my money. I never let anyone know how much I'm carrying.

"If it were Henderson, then he most likely stuck around and watched from a distance when I went to the stage office, then put my satchel on the stage. If that is so, then I'm sure he figured that it was just a matter of getting ahead of the stage and stopping it."

Judd stood. "Any ideas as to where they might have fled

to?"

Ivers shook his head. "As far as I know, Greg Henderson was born and raised in Texas. I can't say about Lars O'Hansen or Manny Wilkes because I never got to know them well enough to know where they came from."

"Thanks for the information, Kurt," Judd said. "We'll see what we can do about locating the culprits, and maybe retrieve some of your money."

Faye and Creed also stood, then they stepped outside with Judd.

Judd said, "Let's go back to the sheriff's office. I've got a few questions for the man."

The sheriff, still seated behind his desk when Judd and the others crowded in, looked up.

Judd walked forward, wanting to let the sheriff know that he'd found out some things that the sheriff had withheld from him. "We found out from Ivers that when he paid off his men, he let three of them go. He gave me their names; said he gave them to you, as well."

Sheriff Hayes merely looked at Judd but did not respond.

Judd then asked, "We were just wondering if you have any leads on those three."

Hayes shook his head. "Nothing as yet, but then I don't make a habit of disclosing all known facts of a case to everyone that walks through the door."

Judd smiled. "We're on your side, Sheriff. Just attempting to get all the information we can before we go looking. I learned from Ivers what the three in question look like but lack a description of Lanie Brooks for when we run across her."

Hayes nodded. "I never met the girl, but others told me

that Miss Brooks is a nice-looking girl about twenty years old, five-foot-two, 110 to 120 pounds in weight. They say that she has blonde hair, blue eyes, and a pretty face."

"Thanks," Judd offered, then he and the others stepped outside.

T.C. wagged his head. "That description fits about half the soiled doves in this town as well as anyplace else out here."

Judd nodded. "At least we now know a little about her."

CHAPTER NINE

"Climb up here with me, pretty lady." Greg extended a hand toward the startled Lanie.

She recoiled and flared a hand. "I can't ride a horse in this dress."

Greg replied, "Not to worry...you won't need it, anyway." He grinned, then said, "Either take the dress off or just hike it up and crawl up here. Come on!" he urged.

Lanie, seeing that she was in no position to argue, stepped forward to stand beside Greg's horse, then lifted her ankle-length dress up to her waist, held it there with one hand, and took Greg's outstretched hand with her other. He pulled her up while swinging her around so she could straddle the horse behind his saddle.

When she was seated, Greg said, "Just wrap your arms around my waist. It's okay to press your titties against my back. I'd like that."

Two hours later, Greg pulled rein near a small creek. "We'll make a camp here," he declared to Manny and Lars. "Lars, if you tend the horses, Manny can scrounge some firewood and the lady and I will set up the camp, get the coffee going."

Lanie did not argue. She slid off the horse's back to stand, then said, "I need to visit the bushes."

Greg nodded. "Just don't be trying to sneak off. I could track you down inside of five minutes."

Lanie declared, "I'm not trying to run off. I mean, I have no place to go. I don't even know where we are. I just gotta pee real badly, then I'll make the coffee."

• • •

Two hours later, things went about as Lanie figured. She had made the coffee, then heated up two cans of beans in a saucepan. Manny had provided the beans from his saddlebags. He opened the cans with a knife he had belted to his side. The three men gobbled plates of beans and some old biscuits and strips of tough, dried jerky.

Lanie contented herself with sipping on a cup of coffee. She was not hungry. It did not matter if she was or not, she knew what was coming a little later and was concerned that they would just do away with her after they were finished using her body. After all, she had witnessed the robbery and the heartless killing of the others. She figured she would only remain alive until they tired of her, which would most likely be tonight, or at least in the next day or so.

In the meantime, she would bide her time and wait. If she could somehow get her hands on a gun or a knife, she would have no problem using the weapon on any one of them; all of them, if possible.

After the meal, Lanie busied herself cleaning the dishes while the men sat around the campfire and swigged busthead whiskey from an unlabeled jug they passed back and forth. Each man scrunched his face when he swallowed the vile liquid. Lanie knew that it would not be long before one of them took her to his bedroll.

A hand grabbed the back of her collar and pulled her to her feet, causing her to drop the cup she was rinsing.

"Them dishes can wait," Greg declared. He then swung her around, took a hand to the front of her dress, and ripped it down the middle. He pulled it off her shoulders so that she stood there nude except for her panties and stockings. He led her to his bedroll then said, "Get 'em off!"

Lanie stepped out of her underpants then went ahead and lay down on the bedroll. Greg merely dropped his pants to his ankles then positioned himself on top of her. She did as she had always done with previous clients, letting her mind go blank as he began to toil.

It seemed as if it took the man a long time to finish, and when he did, he merely rolled off to lie beside her for a few long minutes then remounted her and raped her again. When he was finally sated, he rolled off her again. He called out, "She's all yours, Lars!"

Lars immediately stepped forward. He was nude with his erection at full bloom. "Thought you was gonna keep her all to yourself all night!"

Lars pulled Lanie to her feet then led her to his bedroll a dozen feet away.

On the way, Lanie noticed that Manny was snoring. She figured that maybe there would be one less to worry about tonight. She also noticed that Lars had piled his clothes next to his bedroll—shirt, then pants on top, and the handle of a belted knife tantalizingly sticking out within arm's reach. Lanie centered her mind on the knife, but it was too soon to attempt getting her hand on it. She knew that she needed to bide her time until Greg was asleep. Perhaps Lars would use her for a lengthy time, as well.

Lars wasted no time in crawling on top then entering her and began pumping right away. She turned her head so that she could see Greg lying there on his back, eyes closed. Two minutes passed, which seemed like two hours, then Lars spasmed in his orgasm. She almost cursed because she figured that enough time had not passed for Greg to lose consciousness. She figured to ensure that Lars did not leave just yet, by placing a hand to his back and saying, "You are not done already, are you, big guy?"

Lars still, lying on her, grinned broadly. "Gimme a couple minutes, girl, and I'll take you for a longer ride that you won't soon forget."

Five minutes passed, which seemed to Lanie like an eternity until Lars began to do his business again. Lanie cast her eyes to Greg and saw that his eyelids remained closed. He had most likely passed out or he was deep in slumber.

She looked at the toiling man atop her to see that he had closed his eyes as well. Lanie reached her hand out slowly and took hold of the handle of the sheathed knife. Fortunately, it did not have a keeper thong to hold it in place, and she was able to slide it from the sheath. It had a shiny blade about eight inches long. She hoped that it was sharp enough to do what she now intended.

Lanie darted her eyes around the camp. Both Greg and Manny were asleep, and she thought she could hear both men snoring. She moved her hips a little to keep Lars interested, then brought the knife toward her, positioning its point to the side of Lars's neck.

Lars's eyes blinked open wide when she stabbed, pushing the knife into his neck all the way until the tip of the blade exited the other side. Lar's blood spurted out, dripping onto her own neck and shoulders as he opened his mouth. Lanie, fearful that he might yell out, reached and grabbed Lar's shirt from the pile and covered the man's mouth so that only a weak grunt was the only sound the stricken man made. Lanie began pushing his dead weight to roll off her. She then stood and frightfully looked toward Greg, then to Manny. Both were still snoring.

Now was a critical time. She was unsure of what to do-- whether to take Lars's six-gun and shoot Greg, then Manny, or to use something to coldcock each of them. She knew that she had to do something though, lest they wake up and see what she had done to Lars.

When stepped over to Greg's side, she chose to grab hold of the Winchester lying close by. She took hold of the rifle by the barrel, lifted it over her head, then slammed the butt across the man's face—once, twice, three times before she stopped to see the effect. It was obvious that the blows had caved his nose in, and likely shattered his cheekbones as well.

Greg's arms had moved outward at the first blow, then had fallen to his side. His body twitched, then lay still, as she started to turn to do the same to Manny. But her movement suddenly stopped. Someone had grabbed her from behind. Two arms encircled her, holding her arms close to her sides along with the rifle.

"That's enough!" Manny called out from behind her. "Drop the rifle!" He then asked, "Was you gonna do me next?"

Lanie called out, "Let me go! All I did was to give those bastards what they deserved!"

Manny chuckled. "I don't blame you for doing what you done after seeing what they did to you. My grandmother always said that a man has to pay for his misdeeds at some point in his life."

Manny held her tightly. "Let go of the Winchester," he said again.

"I can't!" Lanie wailed. "You got it pressed against my side!"

Manny loosened his grip, removed his hands from her, and took a half-step back. He then dropped one hand to his six-gun and the other to his side.

Instead of dropping the rifle, Lanie, still having the barrel in her hands, made one step forward then began swinging the rifle around as hard as she could. The loud smacking of the flat side of the rifle stock hitting Manny flush over his left ear was the sound that followed. The man, with both eyes now closed, fell to his right and lay unmoving.

She suppressed the idea of hitting him again. From what she had seen and heard, Manny was not a bad sort, he did not seem to have the killer instinct that Greg and Lars had exhibited. She wondered how he'd come to ride with them. Seeing that he was out of it, she let the rifle fall to the ground.

Lanie didn't care if both the other men were dead; she hoped they were! They were worthless scum and did not deserve to live.

She stepped over to Lars's goods and took the six-gun from his holster, it being a Colt .44. She checked to make sure it had cartridges. She had never shot a large caliber pistol before, but she knew of its workings and figured that she could shoot it if she needed to. She would keep it within arm's reach from now on.

Lanie considered since all of them were dead or unconscious, she could spend the time to go through their saddlebags. After putting her panties back on, she found a shirt in Manny's that fit her well, and a pair of jeans in Lars's bag that was conveniently close to the right waist size. She just had to roll the legs up three folds.

Manny's boots fit her after she donned two pairs of the man's socks. She then saddled Lars's horse, the gray mare that seemed mild-mannered. Walking over to Lars's saddle, she took the carbine from the boot, which also held a Winchester 73. She had previously seen him check and load both weapons, each taking the same .44 cartridges. She grabbed a box and stuffed it into the saddlebags. She deposited the rifle in what was now her saddle boot.

She loaded Greg's saddlebags with the stolen loot inside, added two cans of peaches and some dried jerky—the only foodstuffs that were handy. She added some stick matches, then swung the bags over the mare's back. She then plucked Manny's hat from the man's side and donned it. She rolled a blanket up and tied it behind the saddle.

She then untied both Greg's big black stallion and Manny's pinto and shooed the animals away.

Lanie was exhausted, but she wanted to get away from

here, to put some distance between her and this death camp. She mounted Lars's gray mare and tapped her heels to the animal's sides to get her going, then rode away.

She didn't know where she was but figured to go on to Salina as she had previously planned, rest up, then take the stage on to Kansas City.

She contemplated her situation as she rode along. The bag of money in her saddlebags would now change everything. She didn't have to work with Harlow or anyone else; that was, if she could just hang on to the money.

She would have to wait until daylight to get her directions straight. Until then, all she could do was to just point the horse in what she thought was the right direction. Maybe she would get lucky, locate the road, and just follow it. She hoped she didn't run across any other travelers. It was a dangerous thing for a woman to be riding around the country alone, and she knew too well that there were those who would take advantage if they could.

CHAPTER TEN

When they stepped outside the sheriff's office, Judd and the others walked to their horses

"Do you have any ideas of where to go next, Judd?" T.C. asked.

Judd replied, "Well, since Lanie Brooks has been taken hostage, that changes things. I think we ought to ride out to the robbery site and see what tracks, if any that we can pick up, old and as trampled as they are. Afterward, I don't think there's anything to gain by us traveling north and east any longer—unless, of course, we find tracks going that way.

"As far as I know, those men came from Texas. My gut feeling is that they will head back to familiar territory. If we can locate their trail, I don't mind telling you that I expect to find Miss Brooks's abused body along the way."

T.C. grimaced. "I agree with your assessment of their heading, Judd, but am hopeful that we'll find her alive and well. I will give up the hunt only if we do, indeed, find that Miss Brooks is deceased, but I have no interest in the robbers."

The three of them headed toward the site of the robbery

and located it easily. Torn up ground, evidence of where blood from some of the victims had soaked into the dirt, and some scattered clothing were all easily discernible. There were all kinds of tracks covering the ground, many of which had been made by the posse.

It didn't take long for Judd to study everything, then declare, "Okay, now we know the direction of the trail the posse took, which is still heading northeast." He pointed to his right, then said, "Those robbers did that to throw any trackers off. I believe it a waste of time to follow that trail. If I were the outlaws, I would do as they most likely did, then at an opportune time, I would cut straight south.

"What I propose we should do is to head due east for the rest of the day. Who knows, maybe we'll get lucky and locate three sets of tracks. If we don't locate a trail by day's end, then tomorrow we turn around and head due west. It's my belief that we will find tracks, and at some point, the tracks will turn due south, heading toward Texas. If so, then, depending on how hard they ride, it'll just be a matter of us catching up to them."

They rode due east until the sun went down, but it was still light enough to see for a time yet. Judd held up a hand and pointed straight ahead. "We can make camp over by that creek."

What they found when they got closer was evidence of someone else's camp, but there was no campfire. From his elevated vantage point atop his saddle, Judd could see three separated men lying down; two were perhaps in their bedding, retired for the night. The third was lying on his stomach next to a blanket as if he had rolled off it. He thought it strange that no guard challenged the outsiders. Apparently, none was posted. Two horses were wandering in the distance.

When they had ridden closer, Judd called out, "Hello the camp! We mean no harm, just want to say hello."

When no reply came, they rode closer still, and it was soon evident that the men could no longer reply. They had all been killed.

Judd, Faye, and T.C. dismounted their horses. Judd loosened the keeper thong on his six-gun and placed a hand to the handle, apprehensive as he stepped over to look at the man lying on his stomach. He could plainly see that the man had a huge stab wound to his neck and the amount of blood under and around the body bespoke that the man was dead.

T.C. moved to where Greg Henderson lay in his blankets. He made a quick observation, then called out, "This one's dead. Looks like someone smashed his head in with a club."

Faye walked over to stand over the prone Manny Wilkes, whose face was a bloody mess. She squatted beside the still form, then was startled when it appeared one of his arms twitched in movement. She reached to feel the side of the man's neck for a pulse, then called out, "This one's still alive!"

Both Judd and T.C. rushed to her side. Judd knelt down and felt for a pulse as well. "Yep, he sure is. If we clean this guy up, maybe he'll wake up and tell us what happened here."

Judd glanced at T.C. "If you take care of the horses, T.C., Faye and I will get a fire going. Then we can heat some water."

Faye said, "Just get me some kindling, Judd. There's already a pile of limbs here. I'll get the fire going. I'm sure you want to scout around—hopefully, find the tracks of those responsible for this mess."

Judd soon had some handfuls of pinecones, grasses, and small sticks he piled by the same, now-dead fire ring that had served this camp previously. He then wandered around, finding a tattered and ripped dress lying nearby.

He dropped it near Faye's feet as she squatted by the fire she had gotten going and was adding some larger sticks. "These men may be the ones that took the woman. It looks to me like someone cleaned their clocks for them and left them for dead."

He then circled the camp on foot, hoping that he would not find Lanie Brooks's body lying nearby. He did see where three sets of tracks led in, but only one set of tracks led straight away from the camp. He rounded up the two horses that were grazing a short distance away, figuring they'd have a need for them later on.

When he slowly walked up close, neither of the animals shied away as he held out a hand and allowed both to sniff at a handful of oats he had brought with him. He let each nibble some from his hand as he slipped a rope around each horse's neck. He then led them back to the camp and tied the rope to a tree limb. He gave each a handful of oats to eat while he looked around for tracks.

He located the animals' previous tethering, but there was only the one set of tracks leading away from the camp. It was evident that only one person did the damage to the three men lying in the camp.

Was it Lanie Brooks who had ridden away? If it was her, then she was no innocent soiled dove taken for a ride but a hardened, heartless killer. He needed to reassess his thoughts and opinions of the missing—and now, in his mind—very dangerous woman.

It was now almost fully dark, so tracking was out of the question until daylight. Judd went to his saddlebags and pulled out a quantity of wanted posters. He then walked to the now blazing campfire, then squatted down and began going through the posters. He set one poster to his side, the likeness of Greg Henderson. The bounty was $1500.00—dead or alive; wanted for a string of robberies, as well as two known killings.

It didn't take long to locate another poster with the likeness of the man with the slit throat, Lars O'Hansen, who was wanted for theft and murder, as well. The bounty on his head was set at $800.00.

Judd went through the rest of the posters he had, but failed to locate any that fit the description of the live man. The findings certainly put a wrinkle in their quest to locate Lanie Brooks.

Judd would remind T.C. later of their conversation before he'd agreed to being their hunt for Lanie Brooks. He'd told Creed he'd be turning in wanted men—dead or alive—for the bounty, if the opportunity presented itself. He would break off the hunt long enough to do just that. Turning these men in for the bounties was critical and timely, since the two were deceased. He needed to turn the bodies in to the law and get them signed for before deterioration caused them to be unidentifiable.

If taking the bodies in put T.C. Creed's nose out of joint, too bad. Judd would like to know what went on here... perhaps the live one would revive enough to tell them, but he wasn't about to leave these bodies here when there was money to be had. As far as he knew, the nearest law was back in Ellsworth. Judd figured that if they could get an early start, they could be there sometime perhaps by noon tomorrow.

The one live bandit posed a problem for a hurried trip; right now, the stricken man was in no condition to ride a horse. They would have to rig up a travois to drag along, behind one of the horses he had tied up in order to get the man to a doctor in town—that was, if the fella survived through the night. Judd figured that once they got to town and turned the bodies in, they could resume the hunt for the missing woman right afterward.

• • •

Both Judd and T.C. sat on their butts facing the fire, each with a cup of coffee in hand. Faye knelt beside the unconscious man, bathing his battered face with a dampened cloth.

"I found two sets of overlaid tracks heading off that way." Judd pointed to his left. "That would be the tracks of the horses I brought in. They just wandered around looking for something to eat. There's only one set of tracks heading directly away from this camp. That horse would be carrying Miss Brooks, I believe."

Judd then decided to let the others in on his plan for returning to Ellsworth tomorrow. After that, he turned to T.C. and said, "T.C. maybe you can find a couple of poles we could use for a travois if we need it in the morning. Meantime, I'll wrap up those two bodies in blankets tonight so that we can be ready to ride at first light."

T.C. spoke up. "Judd, what do you think about having Faye return the men to town while you and I continue the hunt and get on those tracks while they're still readable? Like you say, it's going to be slow going pulling that travois, and we didn't encounter anyone along the way, so I'd say she most likely would have no problem getting to town safely."

Faye had heard what T.C. had proposed and cast her eyes to Judd to see his reaction.

"That's out of the question!" Judd responded. "Just because we didn't come across anyone doesn't mean there aren't any miscreants out there. Might be one or more are watching us right now, waiting for a chance to strike. Faye has already had her share of strangers causing trouble. I won't allow that to happen again."

T.C. was quick to answer. "I understand. Then what about if you take those men to town and Faye and I continue the hunt? Her being your sidekick, she most likely can do a fair job of tracking. When you're finished with your business in Ellsworth, you could then catch up to us in a day or so."

Judd shook his head. "Won't work that way, either. Those tracks I found are most likely the killer's. If that happens to be Miss Brooks—as unlikely as it seems—then she's a desperate and dangerous woman. She'd stop at nothing, including murder, to keep on her way. If you did catch up to her, I'd say you're going to have a fight on your hands trying to get her to go along with you so's she can be a witness at a trial that has every possibility of involving and possible incriminating her. Faye and I are a team; where one goes, so does the other," he said in finality.

Judd paused for a moment, then said, "Now, if you want to continue the hunt on your own, Faye and I will see to the disposition of these men. Once that's taken care of, we can then return to assist you—that is, if you still want us to? We could meet up with you, say in Salina, in a few days. I believe that's where the stage was heading when robbed. Could be that Miss Brooks will be there resting up and waiting for the next stage to wherever she intends to go."

T.C. nodded, then said, "Guess I'll think on that for a while, Judd. I'd sure like to hear what that live one has to say...if and when he wakes up."

CHAPTER ELEVEN

Salina was exactly where Lanie had ridden. After stabbing Lars and slamming that rifle butt to Greg's and Manny's heads, her only thoughts were to get away from there. It had not been an easy ride; she was alone and frightened.

She ran things through her mind as she rode along; perhaps she had been in too big a hurry to leave before making sure all those men were dead. On reflection, she was sure that Lars had bled to death from the amount of blood that had poured out of him. But she was not sure that the beating she had given Greg and the one head blow to Manny were enough to kill them. Now, she was having regrets that she did not take the time to shoot each of those bastards, particularly Greg and Lars, to make *sure* they were dead. She didn't know why, but deep down, she hoped that Manny had survived.

Well, at least she had the money they had stolen. From their conversations, there must be close to ten thousand dollars in that bag. She would worry about counting it when she was safely inside a locked hotel room.

Fortunately, Lanie was able to locate the well-traveled road heading east to Salina. At least, she figured that it was the right one, and turned the mare onto it. She jabbed her heels to the animal, pushing it to travel faster. When the mare's coat covered in foam, Lanie had enough sense to realize that the animal needed to rest and cool down. She slowed the mare to a walk for a time until she came to a small creek. She dismounted and loosened the cinch, then took the bit out of the horse's mouth to allow the animal to drink.

She lay on her belly on the bank of the creek then leaned over the water, immersing her face, then drinking her fill. She could use the rest, as well, but intended to keep going. It seemed like a long time had passed when she stood up to leave, but from the sun, she knew it was probably less than an hour since she'd stopped. When she resumed the ride, it was at a more leisurely pace to ensure that the mare would not keel over from exertion.

It was almost nine o'clock that night before she reached Salina. She rode down the main street to a large hotel with a sign identifying the structure as The Salina Inn.

When she stepped inside, she knew that she projected a sorry sight. Here she was, dressed in men's dirty clothing, and her hair a mess. She was bedraggled-looking, but she knew that money would mask her appearance. A bath and new clothes would make a world of difference.

The clerk, a balding, bespeckled, lightweight man of about fifty, confirmed her thoughts when he inquired, "Did you have a long trip, madam?"

"Yes. Yes, I did," Lanie stammered. "I'll need a room with a bath."

"Do you know how long you wish to be with us?" the man questioned with a tone as if he were unsure that she would actually be checking in.

Lanie said, "I'm not certain at this point. I'll know better after I've rested for a time."

The clerk nodded, then announced, "The Salina Inn requires a token cash deposit of $5.00 for all new registrants, ma'am."

Lanie laid a twenty-dollar bill on the counter. "Keep that as my deposit. I'll pay any balance due when I'm ready to check out. Now, sir, I have a saddle horse, a gray mare, out front that is in dire need of some extra care. Can you see to that for me?"

The man bobbed his head. "The Inn has its own livery. I'll have one of the boys come and get the horse. Over at the livery they'll make sure that she'll be given food, water, a rub down, and a close inspection for any recognizable potential problems."

Lanie signed her name in the registry, not even giving thought to using a different name. She held no thoughts of anyone tailing her. She was a woman alone, but that did not bother her in the least. She had a satchel full of money, and would now take it easy and do as she pleased.

"Can I have hot water for a bath delivered to my room? I'd also like for my clothing to be laundered and returned." She couldn't go out and about in this get up, even if it were cleaned and returned, she thought. "Also," she added as an afterthought, "is there someone available who might purchase a suitable dress for me and bring it to my room?"

The clerk bobbed his head. "Yes, of course. My wife is real

good with that sort of thing. Take it out of this?" He nodded at the bill on the counter.

Lanie was very hungry but wanted to clean up first, so she asked, "Does the hotel cater food to guest rooms?"

"Why, yes, of course," the man said, then handed a menu to her. "Just pick out any items you like, and they will be promptly delivered to your room."

She scanned the menu, picking out a steak dinner and coffee, along with a slice of apple pie for dessert.

• • •

She awoke the next morning, refreshed from the food, her leisurely bath, and an undisturbed sleep. She felt good, and was eager to get going. She put on her new, soft green dress that the clerk's wife, Ida Mae, had bought at the mercantile. It fit like it had been made for her. She smiled in pleasure. It felt good to be clean, rested, and…rich.

She then made her way to the dining room and had a leisurely breakfast of hot cakes, bacon, and coffee. She struck up a conversation with the server and learned of where the stage office was located, as well as a business that catered to women's wear. She would need more than one dress—and she could certainly afford it.

After breakfast, Lanie made her way to the stage office and learned that the next stage to Abilene and further east would not be leaving town until mid-morning day after tomorrow and would arrive in Abilene later that afternoon. The clerk told her that the same stage would spend the night in town, then resume further east toward Kansas City the following morning at 8:00 a.m. She went ahead and purchased tickets all the way to Kansas City.

She located a livery and arranged for the owner to send a boy to the hotel for her horse and to see if the livery owner would be interested in purchasing the horse and saddle, as she had no further need of the animal.

She then went back to the hotel and advised the front desk of someone coming for the horse. After checking herself out of the inn, she walked to Milly's Dress Shop where she lavished herself in two outfits of wear she would surely need later.

She then went to Gil's Mercantile where she purchased a .32 caliber pistol bathed in silver, and a box of cartridges. She slipped the small pistol, which was much easier for her to handle than the big one she had been lugging around, into her purse.

Once she had finished shopping, she returned to the livery and sold the horse and outfit for forty dollars to the grinning old man. She knew he was taking advantage of her, just as the last livery owner had, but she did not care, only wanting to see to the animal's care. By that time, she had only to return to the stage depot and await the stage arrival.

CHAPTER TWELVE

It was barely daylight when Faye had awakened to see Judd putting the coffee pot he had just filled with water onto a flat rock to one side of the campfire he had rekindled. Faye had slept in her clothes. She lifted the covering off and sat up as she began putting her boots on.

T.C. Creed emerged from the darkness, where he had gone to take care of his morning business, and moved close to the fire, "Morning, Judd," he offered.

Judd bobbed his head as he muttered, "Morning."

Faye stepped away into the bushes. When she returned a few minutes later, she took a canteen in hand, then knelt beside where Manny Wilkes lay on his back with a blanket to his chin. Faye reached a hand to touch the man's forehead. Satisfied that he felt warm and still alive, she opened the canteen and dribbled some water onto the man's lips. She was startled when Wilkes opened his mouth, then swallowed the water. He then suddenly opened his eyes to glare frightfully at Faye.

"It's okay," she soothed. "You're safe now."

"Who…who are you?" he managed in a raspy voice.

Faye replied, "My friends and I came into your camp last night and found you lying here. You looked to still be alive, so I covered you."

T.C., having heard the talk, hurried to kneel and speak to the prone man. "What happened here?"

Wilkes stared, wide-eyed. "I...I don't know," he stammered. "The woman...I was talking to her when she—she hit me with the butt of a rifle! That's all I know." He quieted and began looking around, perhaps fearful Lanie would return.

"Your two friends are both dead," T.C. said. "Do you know where the woman, Miss Brooks, is?"

Wilkes moved his head slightly. "She was here. Greg took her off the stage. It was him that shot all those people. Me and Lars didn't shoot anyone."

"You three held up the stage just to get the woman?" T.C. asked.

Manny Wilkes stared. "We didn't know or care who was on the stage. We was just after the money."

"What money?" T.C. asked.

Wilkes swallowed. "Greg said it was the herd money that Kurt Ivers was sending out of town."

"How did you know it was on the stage?" T.C. asked.

"Lars and Greg and I signed on to ride for the IB Ranch. We joined up with some regular IB Ranch hands and herded those cattle to town for the sale. When Ivers paid the three of us off and let us go without as much as a thank you, Greg figured the man should have given us more for all the trouble we went through getting those damn cattle up from Texas. It was Greg who had worked for Ivers before, and said he knew the man's ways. Greg said that Ivers would attempt to sneak the money out of town to throw off any would-be thieves. He said Ivers had done such before. We three took turns watching, and sure enough, we saw Ivers put the satchel onto the stage.

"Greg said we ought to go and take the money, teach Ivers a lesson for treating us the way he did. He said we deserved a bonus, and all we had to do was to go and collect what was rightfully ours."

Judd, standing close by, reiterated, "So you three held up the stage, and Greg, alone, you say, did all the shooting; killed everyone—driver, shotgun guard, and three passengers, and took the other passenger, Miss Lanie Brooks, hostage along with the satchel of money?"

Manny nodded. "Yes, it was Greg did all the shootin', and I told him I saw no need for him to kill all those folks."

"What did he say when you told him that?" Judd asked.

"He said, now there were no witnesses."

"You watched him do it, but you didn't do anything to stop him," Judd said.

"There wasn't anything I could do. Greg was a known tough guy, and I knew better than to mess with him. I figured if I tried to do anything to stop him that he'd shoot me too!"

Judd then said, "So, after the robbery, you three rode to here with Miss Brooks along and made a camp. Anyone else show up?" Judd already knew no one else had ridden into the camp, because there were no tracks by any but the two horses, here, and the third, which the killer, Lanie Brooks, had ridden away on.

Wilkes said, "I didn't see anyone come by before I was knocked out. It happened sometime last night, is all I know."

Judd turned to confront T.C. "After breakfast, I figure we'll take this fella and those bodies to the sheriff's office in Ellsworth. Then we can take the shortest route we can find to Salina. We might get lucky and find that Miss Brooks is still there. Now that all her tormentors are done for and she has possession of the money, she may be in no hurry to leave."

Faye cooked some pancakes and side pork while the coffee perked. Judd and T.C. saddled the horses. When finished, T.C. turned to Judd and said, "I think I'll do as you suggested, Judd, and follow after those tracks, while you and Faye take care of your business with the sheriff in Ellsworth. Then, if you would, ride up to Salina. I'll meet you there. It looks to me like that's where she's heading. Even if I locate her, I'll still need assistance to get her to Wichita for the trial."

Judd nodded. "I understand. After all, that's why you hired us to begin with. Today is Tuesday. It'll take us a good part of the day today to get to Ellsworth unless Wilkes can ride a horse, which would be faster than pulling a travois along. Once we get to Ellsworth and get Wilkes and these bodies turned in, Faye and I should be able to make a few miles back this way before we camp for the night. Even if we ride all day tomorrow, we still most likely won't get to Salina until Thursday morning. Now, if that suits you, we'll plan on it."

T.C. nodded. "I'll be there. I don't know the town, so I have no idea where we could plan to meet."

"Salina isn't that big that you could get lost. If I remember, there are two decent hotels and a few ratty ones. We'll find you."

T.C. nodded. "Sounds good to me. I'll help you break camp, then I'll be off."

After breakfast, Judd and T.C. loaded both blanketed bodies onto Greg's big black stallion. The animal looked strong enough to haul the extra weight without a problem. Judd then stepped over to Manny, who was sitting on his butt and still sipping coffee. "You think you can ride, or do we need to rig up a travois?"

Manny stared for a moment, then said, "No need for no damned travois. I can ride."

Judd nodded. "Okay, then let's go." He escorted Manny over to the pinto, had him mount, then tied the man's hands to the saddle horn. Judd took the pinto's reins and wrapped them around the saddle horn. He looped a rope around the pinto's neck and tied the end to his own saddle horn. He then handed the stallion's reins to the now-mounted Faye. "I'll lead the way with the prisoner; you can ride alongside or follow with the bodies."

Faye bobbed her head in acknowledgement. She waited until Judd gigged his horse forward, then fell in behind the pinto.

• • •

They arrived in Ellsworth around noontime. Judd rode straight to the sheriff's office, then pulled out the wanted posters on both Greg Henderson and Lars O'Hansen. He did not have a poster on Manny Wilkes; he was in hopes that perhaps the sheriff had one. If nothing else, Manny alone would answer for the robbery and murders of the stage occupants—regardless of his whining that he was innocent of the killings.

The sheriff, having seen the arrival of the blanket-clad bodies, stepped outside to confront Judd.

After a brief explanation, Judd lifted the blanket covering Greg Henderson and held the man's head up by his hair. Henderson's face, beaten, with the nose mashed in and streaked in dried blood, made it hard to recognize. It took a while before the sheriff nodded that the deceased matched the wanted poster that Judd had handed him.

The two men then identified the remains of Lars O'Hansen. Judd moved to the horse carrying Manny Wilkes. Judd cut the rope holding Manny's wrists to the saddle horn. Wilkes grimaced, perhaps in resignation of his fate, and slowly stepped down.

The sheriff, with a hand on his pistol butt, pointed to the jailhouse door. "In there!" he commanded.

Wilkes stepped through the door, followed by the sheriff, then Judd. Faye followed a step behind. After he locked Wilkes in a cell, the sheriff walked into the office where the two waited. He took a chair behind his desk. "Damned fine work, Judd, you and Faye catching up to 'em and bringing them in. Did you locate the money as well?"

Judd figured it was best to come clean. "Faye and I did not kill those men, sheriff, we found them already deceased. We're just turning the bodies in for the bounties on them."

It took a while for Judd to explain that he believed Lanie Brooks was a passenger on the stage and abducted by the three robbers that they were now turning in, the men who did the actual robbery and killings. He figured Lanie Brooks had somehow killed Henderson and O'Hansen, and had knocked cold the prisoner, Manny Wilkes. He believed that she took the money and fled to who-knew-where, but her tracks headed toward Salina. Judd emphasized the fact that they were returning to her trail as soon as they finished here.

The sheriff nodded his head in understanding. "You two have been busy with all this detective work. I can alert Marshal Clegg over in Salina by telegraph; he could keep an eye out and pick her up when she shows up. I don't know of any charges we could make on her, if she's the one who killed those wanted men, but at least she could tell us how all those folks on the stage were killed and we'd soon find out if she has the stolen money in her possession."

Judd cut his eyes to the sheriff. "If it's all the same to you, Sheriff, I'd rather you not do that just yet. For one thing, we need her alive so that she can give testimony at a trial to be held later in Wichita. And two, the law in Salina, not knowing her recent past history of violence, might find that despite her innocent looks, she'd resort to shooting one or more of them in order to keep the money. If, by chance, they returned fire and happened to fatally hit her, all our efforts to secure a witness for the trial would be in vain."

Judd paused for a moment, then continued. "We already have a man headed to Salina. If he can locate her, he'll keep a watch on her movements until we get there to assist. It's our intention to detain her for the same reasons that you outlined and see that she attends the trial. Of course, if she does have the money, we'll see to its return to the rightful owner."

The sheriff, seemingly unsure of what Judd just outlined, furrowed his forehead. After a long, silent moment, he said,

"You got two days."

A little later, Judd and Faye had a quick meal at Margie's Café, then headed their horses toward Salina. It was a good seventy-something miles to go, and they would not make it today. They'd ride until darkness forced them to stop and make a camp. By that time, the horses would need rest, water, and feed.

It was past dark when Judd held up a hand, then said, "The horses need to rest for a time, so let's throw down here till daylight."

• • •

The next morning, Faye awakened to the smell of coffee brewing on a small fire while Judd was busy saddling both their horses. She knew Judd would be frothing at the bit to get going. She rolled out of her blankets and pulled on her breeches, shirt, and boots, then began rolling up the bedding.

They exchanged morning greetings then sat and sipped coffee from their tin cups.

"Do you think we'll get there before dark tonight, Judd?" Faye asked.

"Yeah, I figure we got thirty or so miles to go. If we get going, we ought to be in town mid- to late afternoon. Then, of course, we need to locate T.C. and see if he has found Miss Brooks. Plenty of things to think about. If she decided to leave town and he followed her, then we'd be on a cold trail."

They each ate a cold biscuit with their second cup of coffee. Afterward, Judd kicked dirt onto the dying fire. They mounted up and headed out.

It was near to four o'clock when Judd's and Faye's

lathered and tired horses entered Salina.

Judd pointed down the main street. "Let's go down to The Salina Inn on the right, there. We can get a room, get these animals taken care of, then start looking for T.C."

CHAPTER THIRTEEN

Wonderment—then concern—entered Lanie Brooks's mind while dining. She had glanced across the dining room to see an older man seated alone at a table; he seemed to be staring at her, then quickly averted his eyes when she looked in his direction.

On reflection, it was not the first time she had seen the man, but now was the first time she paid close attention. She didn't remember ever having met him before, although she had been used by more than one faceless, older man in her past as a prostitute.

This man had not bothered her, but it was mysterious how he had glanced away when she looked in his direction. She knew she was attractive. It seemed to be the nature of almost all men, old and young alike, upon catching her eye, to smile broadly and eventually make their way over to her table. But this man did not do that.

Was he a spy for some law office, or did he somehow know about the money? Was he waiting for others to join him before confronting her?

After the filling meal, and seeing that the man was still

seated at his table, she quietly left the room. She approached the inn's clerk's window and slid a twenty-dollar bill across the check-in desk. "I'd like to know if anyone has been here asking about me," she said with a smile.

The clerk stared at her for a moment, seeming to digest that she was offering him a very generous reward for what was nothing more than a little information. He reached over and slid the bill toward himself. "Why, yes, ma'am, there was an older gentleman...one of our guests, in fact. He inquired if Lanie Brooks was a guest at the hotel as well? We strive to accommodate all our guests, so I let him know that you were, indeed, a guest. He also most likely saw your name in the register when he signed in." He spun the register and put a finger on the name of Thomas Creed. "That's the man's signature."

Lanie nodded. "How long has he been here?"

"He came in yesterday. Didn't say how long he'd be here."

"Thank you," Lanie offered, then turned and walked toward her room. She rolled the name Thomas Creed around in her mind, attempting to remember where she had heard that name before. Perhaps it would come to her later. In the meantime, she figured it would be best to leave town and put some distance between her and this mysterious man. She intended to use a different name from now on. Her freedom and the money were at stake, and she intended to keep both.

She knew she should leave without anyone's knowledge of her departure, particularly the blabby clerk's—but that posed a problem. The stage was not scheduled to leave until tomorrow, but she wouldn't wait that long. She went to her room and quickly changed into a cotton blouse and loose-fitting pleated skirt that would be fit for travel. She would leave her other newly purchased clothing here and not check out, so as not to alert the clerk of her departure.

When she stuffed all the money into her purse, it bulged a little too much, so she took five bundles of the cash and secured them flat around her middle, under her blouse.

She was careful when she left her room and walked past the clerk's desk. Fortunately, the man had his back turned away and was fiddling with the leg of an overturned chair, so didn't see her. Not wanting to be obvious, and possibly under scrutiny of the mysterious older man or others, she walked down the street to Milly's Dress Shop that she had patronized yesterday. The dress shop owner, the man at the mercantile, and the livery owner were the only people she had conversed with other than the hotel clerk. Of the group, she figured this woman, Milly, would be the only one she could possibly trust to be mum about her activities, so she stepped inside.

Milly, a woman fifty years of age, slight of build with her graying hair in a tight bun atop her head, projected the image of a caring mother. The woman's demeanor was attractive to Lanie.

Milly immediately recognized her recent customer. She smiled a greeting and said, "You look great in your new outfit—"

Lanie cut her off by saying, "Thank you, Milly. I just stopped to see if I could possibly ask a favor of you."

Milly smiled at her. "I'd be happy to oblige, if I can."

Lanie put a stern look on her face, then said, "I believe

that a man, whom I do not know, has been following me... for what reason, I am unsure of. I want to leave town without that man or anyone else being aware of my departure. It would take hours for me to explain to you how and why I am in this predicament and feel the need to leave.

"Right now, I just want to sneak out of town unseen by anyone. The problem is that I already sold my horse, and I bought a ticket on the stage to Topeka—but because of circumstance, I cannot wait for the stage. I fear the man will observe and follow. Woman to woman, I am asking for your advice and possible assistance..."

Milly stood wide-eyed while listening to Lanie's tale of woe, and her predicament. When it appeared Lanie was finished, Milly was silent for a long moment, perhaps still digesting the request, and then she said, "Not to worry, Lanie. I don't need to know all the details. I believe everyone, including myself, has something in their past that they would go to great lengths to keep from becoming public knowledge. Now, tell me, do you think that the man shadowing you observed your coming here?"

Lanie shook her head. "He was still in the dining room when I stepped away to come here, and I don't believe that he saw me leave the hotel."

Milly, somber-faced, said, "Good. Now, here's what I believe might work to get you out of town. You can remain here, unseen in my back room. Shird, my handy man, always brings my buggy to pick me up at closing time, which is 6:00 p.m. He always pulls up out back. The buggy is a two-seater. We can easily hide you behind the front seat, covered in a blanket, when we leave town. Usually, no one takes notice, as most folks are anxious to get to their own homes for the evening. It's only a couple of miles to my place, and you're welcome to spend the night. I live alone, other than Shird taking care of the place, since my husband passed on a year-and-a-half ago. I would love the company. You need not be concerned about Shird; he is a harmless bachelor of seventy years, and content to live in the barn with the animals.

"The stage conveniently passes on the road right out in front. Tomorrow morning, Shird can be standing out front when the stage comes along and wave the driver to stop. He has done that before when my sister was ready to leave, after a visit, this past spring. Since you already have a ticket, you can board and be on your way."

Lanie was flabbergasted as she stared at Milly. "I don't know what to say, Milly, other than thank you. You have no idea what this means to me."

CHAPTER FOURTEEN

Judd and Faye began walking their animals down the main street when up ahead a man stood in the middle of the street facing them and began waving his arms. As they got closer, Judd could see that T.C. was the man doing the waving.

When Judd and Faye had ridden to within a dozen feet of T.C., he called excitedly, "She's here! I've been watching her. She's staying at the Inn. I saw her signature in the registry book when I checked in. She's not afraid of using her own name, so that tells me she's unaware of anyone tailing her. I didn't think it wise to approach her until you two got here, but I would have if she attempted to leave."

"Is she alone?" Judd asked.

T.C. nodded. "She's been keeping to herself, dining alone, then returning to her room. It appears that she is just waiting for the stage to Abilene, scheduled to leave tomorrow morning around 10:00 a.m. The clerk over at the depot said that she had purchased a ticket to Topeka."

"Good work, T.C. Looks like things are working in our favor. Faye and I need to get these animals cared for, check in at the hotel, then clean up and rest for a spell before dinner."

"The Inn has its own livery," T.C. cut in. "I'll take your horses around back while you two check in. Then I'm going back on the watch. Last I saw of her, she had lunch, then left, and I believe that she returned to her room. As far as I know, she's still there. You never know, though; if she got wind of us pursuing her, she'd most likely attempt to sneak away. I'll see you two later. Meet you, say, at six for dinner in the dining room there in the Inn."

• • •

At 6:00 p.m., Judd and Faye entered the large dining room, then headed to a table against the back wall where T.C. Creed sat with a drink glass in hand.

T.C. waited until the two were seated, then said, "I haven't seen her since lunch, but she'll most likely be coming in for her evening meal before long."

The server stepped to the table to see of the couple's drink wants. "Just coffee for me," Judd said. Faye said, "That's what I want, as well."

An hour later, the three had just finished a full meal of pork chops, mashed potatoes, green beans, a garden salad, and bread when the server reappeared with three slices of apple pie on saucers arranged in her hands. She set a slice before each of them, refilled their coffee cups, then walked away.

T.C. could see that Judd was growing uneasy because there had been no sign of Lanie Brooks coming into the room for dinner. T.C. rolled his shoulder. "Can't imagine what's keeping her, she was here last night right at six."

"Perhaps she found another place to dine," Faye offered.

Judd nodded, then said, "I guess we could wander around and see if she's out and about, but it could be that she's just holed up in her room, resting up before tomorrow's stage ride."

After an hour of scouring all the other establishments, eateries, and saloons, Judd said, "Guess we'll have to wait until morning. As long as we're up early, one of us is bound to see her when she comes down for breakfast."

"I'll be in the dining room soon as it opens," T.C. declared as the three entered the Inn. They then separated to their rooms.

• • •

An hour later, T.C. lay wide-awake despite having made every attempt to sleep. He was chagrined at not being able to point out the elusive young woman to Judd and Faye. He immediately knew who she was when she had first walked into the hotel's restaurant. He now was sorry that he had not confronted her at that time. Was there a chance that she had slipped away right under his nose? It plagued him to wonder. He tossed and turned for half the night until he finally fell asleep a little after midnight.

It was a little past daylight when a knock sounded at T.C.'s door. He rolled groggily out of bed, then called out, "Yes!"

"Just checking to see if you were sleeping in," Judd said from the hallway.

"I'll be right there!" T.C. replied.

A little later at the breakfast table, after T.C. had sat down, Faye said, "Hasn't been a lone female enter since I came down, and I was here when they opened the restaurant's door."

T.C. nodded. "Thanks for being on the lookout. I didn't go to sleep until late. Surely, she'll be coming in shortly."

They sat apprehensively during breakfast, each of the three casting frequent glances to the entrance as other patrons and guests arrived. But Lanie Brooks was not one of them.

Judd spoke up. "Let's go see the clerk at the front desk and see if she possibly checked out and slipped away."

When asked, the clerk shook his head. "No, Miss Brooks is paid up, but I haven't seen her since yesterday morning. I believe she had said she would be leaving on the stage this morning. I expect she'll be along any time now."

Faye stepped forward. "Would it be possible for us to check her room and see if she's alright? We're worried about her."

The clerk turned. "Go ahead and knock on her door, room twelve. If she doesn't answer, then see Agnes. She's upstairs cleaning rooms right now. Just tell her I said it's alright, and she'll open the door to room twelve so you can check. She'll want to make the bed, anyway."

The three hustled upstairs and knocked on the door. Having received no reply, they turned and found Agnes, a slight woman with her hair tightly packed under a knotted scarf above her ears. She was just stepping away from room eight, pulling along a mop bucket on rollers.

When Faye explained, Agnes dropped the handle of the mop bucket and stepped to room twelve. She tapped on the door three times and called out, announcing her presence. "Cleaning lady," she said. When she received no reply, she looked at Faye. "I don't believe anyone's in there." She then took a skeleton key, fitted it into the lock, and opened the door.

Agnes stepped into the room and looked around as Judd, Faye, and T.C. crowded in behind her.

"The room's pretty much the way I left it yesterday," Agnes offered. "That bed hasn't been slept in, but her clothes are still here. I won't do any cleaning until later...maybe she'll be back."

Faye thanked the woman, then she, Judd, and T.C. walked away.

Outside, Judd stopped and said, "All we can do is to wait over at the stage depot—see if she shows. Although, I got a hunch that, for whatever reason unknown to us, she's already left town."

When the stage arrived, they surrounded it in anticipation. A young couple stepped forward and boarded the stage, but no Lanie Brooks. They watched as the driver got the stage rolling and disappeared out of town.

"What do we do now?" T.C. asked.

"Let's check all the places she was known to patronize yesterday one more time," Judd said.

• • •

The livery owner wagged his head. "I bought a hoss off her, but she hasn't been back."

The mercantile owner reaffirmed that the described young woman did a little shopping day before yesterday but had not returned.

Milly at the dress shop said, "Good customer, that Lanie. She stopped in yesterday afternoon and showed me how well one of her new outfits fit her. Said she was catching the stage today. Might be that you just missed her since I saw the stage leave a while ago."

Back outside, Judd said, "We've scoured the town enough to know that she's not here. I believe we ought to get on the road to Topeka and take up the hunt there."

CHAPTER FIFTEEN

Things had gone exactly as Milly had outlined for Lanie. The handy man, Shird, showed up out back of the shop at five minutes to 6:00 p.m. Milly stepped out first, looked around, then motioned for Lanie to climb onto the carriage and to lie on the floor behind the front seat. She then covered Lanie, who had curled into a ball, with a blanket. Once out of sight of any eyes in town, Milly called out, "You can sit up now, Lanie, we're clear of town."

A little while later, Shird pulled the carriage to the front of Milly's home and waited until both women had stepped to the ground before driving it to the barn situated not far behind the house.

For the most part, Lanie shared a delightful evening with Milly. The two, despite Milly's objections that she did not need help, fixed and enjoyed a simple meal consisting of a fresh green salad, some leftover pot roast, and mashed potatoes.

Milly had not asked about Lanie's past but did ask where she was going. Lanie offered voluntarily, "I don't have any family that I'm attempting to locate, but I once spent some time in Kansas City and met some delightful people there. I happen to have recently come into some money, and am interested in possibly opening a business there."

Milly listened with interest, yet she was taken aback a bit. Here this attractive young woman was, obviously running away from something in her past, perhaps a failed marriage, yet she seemed optimistic in telling of her intentions for the future. Still, she was hesitant in revealing what circumstance was driving her to sneak out of town.

The mystery was intriguing to Milly, so she asked, "Why do you believe that someone is after you, Lanie? And who do you think it is?"

Lanie stared at her for a moment as if to remain mum, then she took a breath and relented. She began by telling of her poor home life, then of meeting George Wiggins. "He wooed me, and I fell in love with him. He promised he would marry me, so I quit my job and left town with him. I thought he was a sales representative of some sort. We began traveling from one town to the next. I was beginning to wonder when and where we would marry and settle down. It only took a short time, a couple of weeks, for his true intentions to come forth. I was blind to the fact that he did not have a profession other than gambling.

"I sat by while he gambled, and I did not argue when he began pushing drinks on me. He told me the drinks would help me to relax, and I would feel better. Well, things got out of hand one evening after I had one too many drinks. I was very tipsy, and George jumped at the opportunity to use me to make some money. He sent a stranger to my table and nodded encouragement as the man openly fondled me, then led me to my room and used my body. From that night on,

George readily expected me to whore out in every town we visited. He said I needed to do my part in our support.

"Of course, my attitude toward him soured. One night, down in Great Bend, I was having a drink with a young cowboy when George, believing my time wasted, stepped forward in an attempt to send me to a man whom he said was waiting for me. The cowboy took offense and protested. He and George had words, and the cowboy drew his six-gun. It ended up that he shot George in the chest. I saw an opportunity to part with George's lying and cheating ways, so I left town."

She paused for a moment, then continued. "I drove George's buggy to Ellsworth and spent the night, then caught the stage to Salina. My luck would not hold for long, though. Three no-accounts held up the stage a few miles out of town. One of them shot and killed the driver, shotgun guard, and several passengers—everyone who was on the stage except for me. They took a satchel off the stage, then took me with them. They made a camp and began drinking a lot of whiskey.

"Later that night, one of them raped me. When he was sated, he then called to his partner that it was his turn to have me. I figured that when they all had their fill of me, they would just shoot me and leave my body for the scavengers.

"If there was a way, I needed to get away from them by any means possible. When the second busied himself on top of me, I managed to locate his knife, got it in hand, and used it to stick him in the throat. I muffled his cry as he died. I slid out from under him then took his rifle in hand and used it to bash the leader of the group's head in. I also cold cocked the third one, but I don't think I hit him hard enough to kill him.

"I saddled one of the horses, took the satchel of money, and left the camp. Now, I'm fearful that that third one, whom I knocked out, is on my trail. I am also fearful that the law may be on my trail, looking for the money those three killers had taken off the stage."

Milly was flabbergasted at what this young innocent-looking woman had confessed to her.

She felt sorry for her, wondering if there was anything she could do to help Lanie. After a moment of contemplation, she then decided to offer the young woman a suggestion that could lead to her putting her life in some semblance of order.

"Lanie, you've certainly had a rough go of things. Some of us—most of us, in fact, have difficulties throughout our lives. Recognizing and doing the right thing can be a challenge to even a strong-willed person." She paused for a moment, then continued. "The money you have in your possession is ill-gotten and will only bring you continued misery. Look at what it has done to you already. I believe that, for your own good, you should turn the money in to the sheriff in town and get rid of that hindrance. You can stay here with me for a time until you can re-situate yourself. I could use some help down at the dress shop. I've been thinking of hiring someone."

Lanie wrinkled her forehead when she looked at Milly. "I'll think about it, Milly. That is very kind of you to offer. I really appreciate your thoughts, and going out of your way to help me, as well. For now, though, I still intend to catch that stage."

CHAPTER SIXTEEN

T.C. was quite excited when Judd and Faye rode into town. He thought it would be a simple matter for the three to approach Lanie Brooks, perhaps in the dining room, and then disclose that it was their intent to escort her to Wichita for the trial. Instead, she had disappeared. He was chagrined that the girl had slipped away, despite his watching her closely. She was on the move, and obviously more elusive than he had imagined.

The three rode out of town. At Judd's suggestion, they took the road eastward toward Abilene, since that was where Lanie Brooks had purchased a ticket for. It was late in the day, almost dark, when they arrived. It was full dark by the time they had seen to their animals' care and checked into The Premiere Hotel.

Faye asked if the dining room was still open. The clerk indicated that it would seat diners until 9:00 p.m. They made their way into the large room to see several diners just finishing their meals and leaving. They ordered drinks and a meal and discussed what they should do in the morning.

"I feel that we should scour the town; check all the hotels

and such first thing after breakfast," Judd offered. "If we don't get a lead early on, then we might as well continue on toward Topeka."

The three spent the night, then met at the restaurant's door at the agreed upon time of 5:00 a.m. when the eatery opened. They took seats at a requested back-of-the-room table and were served coffee. From the table's vantage point, they could observe anyone coming in. It did not take long for the restaurant to begin filling up as sleepy diners, eager to get their day started, took seats and ordered coffee.

After Judd, Faye, and T.C. had finished eating and were supping their third cup of coffee, it was full daylight outside. Judd was anxious to get going when suddenly T.C.'s hand touched his shoulder. "There she is!" he muttered. "She just came in."

Judd and Faye glanced around to see the waitress escorting a young woman in a pleated skirt to a small table to the group's right.

"I won't let her get away this time," T.C. declared.

Judd nodded. "The place is busy, and I don't think she noticed us here. No reason to do anything yet unless she recognizes you, T.C. Let's take our time, let her get situated, and then we can move in."

Ten minutes later, Judd said, "Alright, I believe we can go over and confront her now."

Faye shook her head. "I'll go over and talk to her...see if she is willing to go along."

Judd looked at her for a moment, then nodded. "Alright. Just keep in mind that she has a gun and might be willing to use it. T.C. and I will be right here, just in case."

Faye nodded, then walked across the room to stand before the table next to a large window where Lanie Brooks sat.

"Lanie?"

Lanie whipped her head around to stare wide-eyed at the young woman who was just a few years older than she was. "Yes?" she replied.

Faye held a hand toward a chair across from Lanie, "May I?"

Lanie nodded. Faye took a seat, then introduced herself. "I'm Faye McJunkin. My associates, Mister Judd Jacoby and Mister T.C. Creed, are seated across the room, there." She hooked a thumb in that direction.

Lanie glanced over to the two men, holding her eyes on T.C. Creed for a long moment, then returned her gaze to Faye. She sat silently.

"Lanie, Judd and I are bounty hunters. We've been employed by Mister Creed to find and escort you to Wichita for an upcoming trial. Mister Creed's son, Larry, has been charged with murdering a man—a man you were associated with...a Mister George Wiggins."

Lanie frowned. "I know him, all right, and I had hoped that I'd never see that rat again."

Faye looked at the table, then said, "Well, you don't have to worry about that, because he's dead. As we understand it, Wiggins died from a gunshot wound that came from Larry Creed's six-gun. Larry says that you were there, standing right behind him, and witnessed the shooting. He said you might possibly have pushed his arm and caused the weapon to fire."

Lanie nodded. "I heard the shot and saw him fall to the

floor—so what?"

Faye stared across the table into Lanie's eyes. "Mister Creed feels that your testimony at Larry's trial could make a difference in what kind of sentence Larry receives. He could get either some jail time, or, at the most, a death sentence. Without any other witnesses to call, your testimony could make the difference; otherwise, Larry will most likely receive the death penalty. Mister Creed has gone to great lengths to locate you. The man is just doing what he can to save his son's life."

Lanie shook her head. "I didn't know that cowboy before the shooting. I never laid eyes on him before. He came into the saloon where I was working and bought me a drink. If he walked in right now, I'm not sure I can even remember what he looks like. I don't see how my going to the bother of attending a trial and telling what I saw would make a difference. I'm not interested." She then turned her head to stare at the table, perhaps hoping that Faye would just go away.

Faye remained silent for a moment, then said, "Well, Lanie, I'm afraid that we—my associates and I—must insist that you accompany us to Wichita in time for the trial, whether you want to or not. If you do not come willingly, then you will be tied and forced to make the trip."

Lanie glared at Faye. "Am I under arrest?" she fumed.

Faye nodded. "In a way, yes, you are. We intend you no harm, and it would be easier on you if you came along with us willingly."

Lanie reached a hand toward her purse.

Faye spoke up. "We know you have a gun, Lanie, but it will do you no good to bring it out. Judd is watching closely, and he would not hesitate to shoot you, if you brandish it."

Lanie stayed her hand, then said, "I know this is all about the money. Why don't you just take it and leave me alone!"

Faye glared across the table at the troubled young woman. "Oh, the money from the stage robbery will be returned to its rightful owner, which will be a credit to you, but it has nothing to do with Larry Creed's trial."

• • •

While Judd escorted Lanie and Faye to check out of their respective rooms, T.C. rushed to the telegraph office. He sent a telegram to lawyer William Jenkins, letting the man know that Lanie Brooks was in his custody, and inquired if a trial date had been set in Wichita.

It was mid-morning before T.C. received confirmation that the trial was set to begin on July 19, exactly one week away.

A short time later, he, Judd, and Faye escorted Lanie Brooks from the hotel to a waiting buggy that Judd had purchased for the two women to ride in while he and T.C. follow closely on their horses. Using the buggy would make it a more pleasant journey for the women than by horseback, but it would also make the trip to Wichita slower than if they all rode horses. Since the trial was a week away, they had plenty of time to get to Wichita to attend.

EPILOGUE

It took five days for the group to make the trip to Wichita. They stopped into the Abilene sheriff's office long enough to turn over the cash taken from the stage. It amounted to over $9600.00. Lanie had managed to go through near to four hundred dollars in her short, but extravagant, spending spree. Judd insisted any rewards for the return of the money, which usually amounted to ten percent of the retrieved funds, go to the young woman.

After arriving in Wichita, it was two days later that the court was convened for Larry Creed's trial. T.C. stood and requested to address the court. Judge Winifred McDougal granted him permission to do so.

T.C. then told of the presence of Lanie Brooks, the soiled dove his son Larry had proclaimed pushed his arm, causing his six-gun to discharge and killing George Wiggins.

T.C. requested that Lanie Brooks be a witness to the court since she had testimony not previously heard. The judge granted the request.

When called to explain her relationship to Larry Creed, Lanie stood and tearfully explained that she did not know the defendant personally. She had met him at the saloon that day and was having a pleasant drink with him when George approached the table. She hesitated until Lawyer Jenkins stood and spoke up. "I believe the judge would like to hear your version of what happened next, Miss Brooks."

Lanie paused for a moment in the silence of the courtroom and cast her eyes away from the judge's glare. She began by telling that when Larry Creed pulled his six-gun on George Wiggins, she had reacted by pushing against his arm.

"I am not sorry that George was shot. He deceived me and turned me into a whore! If I had the gun in my own hand, I would have gladly pulled the trigger. George was a no-account son of a bitch, and he deserved to die!"

After her testimony, the judge rapped his gavel. "In view of the witness's testimony, Lanie Brooks is to be taken into custody for willfully aiding in the death of George Wiggins. The court will recess for one hour while this new evidence is considered."

At the end of an hour, the judge returned to the bench and called the court to order.

"The defendant, Larry Creed is to rise and face the bench." When he did so, the judge continued. "Larry Creed, it is decreed by this court that the charge of first-degree murder against you be dismissed; however, since a loaded and cocked six-gun in your hand was discharged unintentionally, resulting in the death of George Wiggins, the court finds you guilty of the charge of involuntary manslaughter. This is a serious charge for a violent offense. It is the sentence of this court that you serve no less than thirty-four months incarceration for this crime." He smacked his gavel to the desk pad then said, "The court calls the defendant, Lanie Brooks to face the bench."

When a bailiff escorted her to do so, the judge began. "Lanie Brooks, the court finds that, by your own admission, you caused Larry Creed's six-gun to fire for the purpose of causing harm to the deceased George Wiggins. This is a serious charge of manslaughter, whether voluntary or involuntary. The court finds that your action was not premeditated; therefore, the charge against you is involuntary manslaughter, the same as Mr. Creed. By law, you are entitled to legal counsel. If you wish legal counsel, then the court will adjourn, and your case will be tried at a later date."

He paused for a moment, then said, "If, however, you decline legal counsel, sentencing will follow promptly." The judge raised an eyebrow as he awaited Lanie's reply.

Lanie did not need to think about it. She wanted this whole nightmare to end as quickly as possible. She saw no benefit in waiting in a jail cell until the judge could reschedule a trial that she was bound to lose, anyway. Lanie replied, "I do not want any legal counsel, sir."

The judge relaxed slightly, seemingly relieved by her choice to end the proceedings today. He wasted no time before beginning.

"Lanie Brooks, it is the sentence of this court that you be detained and incarcerated for the period of thirty-four months, as prescribed by law."

He banged his gavel onto his wooden pad on the desk, indicating the trial was over.

Judd and Faye, along with T.C., filed out of the

courtroom. Judd and Faye had stayed in town to attend the trial out of curiosity.

T.C. shook hands with Judd, then extended his hand to Faye and shook her hand, as well.

"I'm satisfied that the judge is an honorable man and serving the court well. I thank both of you for helping me locate and bring Lanie Brooks to testify. Without her testimony, you can well imagine what Larry's sentence would have been. Now that this job is complete, what do you folks have in mind to do? Are you going to return to your ranch for a rest?"

Judd smiled. "Actually, T.C., we've had enough of a rest. It's time for us to get back to what we do best. We checked in with the sheriff just this morning and picked up a couple of wanted posters on two men who robbed a bank over in Pratt, just west of here. We're going to head over and see if we can pick up a trail."

ABOUT THE AUTHOR

J.L. (Jerry) Guin spent a hitch in the U.S. Navy, then spent 25 years as a lumber salesman for various distributors on the north coast of northern California.

He wrote his first book, Matsutake Mushroom, in 1997. He then turned to writing western fiction. So far, he has over 40 short stories in print under the name of Jerry Guin, and 16 western novels under the name of J.L. Guin. Early on, he became a member of Western Writers of America and Western Fictioneers.

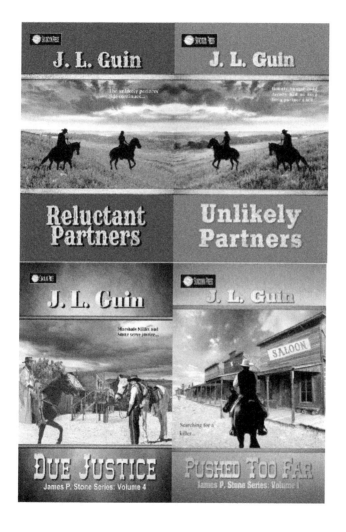

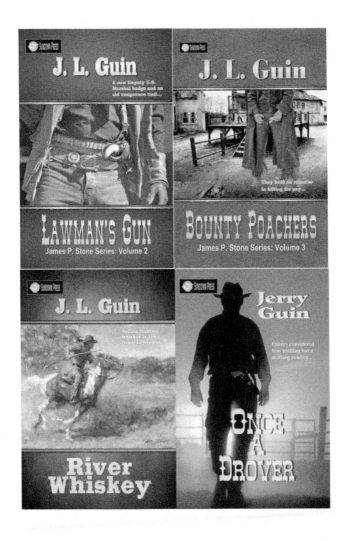

Made in the USA
Middletown, DE
08 February 2022